CAJUN STORIES MY GRANPA TOLE ME

CAJUN STORIES MY GRANPA TOLE ME

Tommy Joe Breaux

PELICAN PUBLISHING COMPANY
Gretna 1999

Library of Congress Cataloging-in-Publication Data

Breaux, Tommy Joe.
Cajun stories my granpa tole me / Tommy Joe Breaux.
p. cm.
ISBN 1-56554-416-1 (alk. paper)
1. Cajuns—Louisiana—Breaux Bridge—Anecdotes. 2. Cajuns—Louisiana—Breaux Bridge—Humor. 3. Breaux Bridge (La.)—Social life and customs—Anecdotes. 4. Breaux Bridge (La.)—Social life and customs—Humor. 5. Breaux family—Anecdotes. 6. Breaux family—Humor. I. Title.
F379.B75B75 1999
976.3'48—dc21
98-56059
CIP

Illustrated by Dominicus Maters

Printed in Canada

Published by Pelican Publishing Company, Inc.
1000 Burmaster Street, Gretna, Louisiana 70053

This book is dedicated to my two grandfathers: Granpa "Fiddlin' Pete," whose talent was passed on to me to make the stories Granpa Gilbert told me come to life. It is also dedicated to my two children, Katie and Jason, who have always made me proud to be called their dad; and to my wife, and best friend, Cathy, who gave them to me. I love y'all dearly. I also give thanks and dedicate this book to the good Lord, who provided me with a wonderful family, great friends, and a Cajun sense of humor.

CONTENTS

FOREWORD

In the unwritten rules of teenage ritual is a law that states that any family trip that interferes with an active social life is both boring and pointless. In other words, if I have something to do and Dad plans a trip that I really don't want to go on, I am required, by nature, to dislike each and every aspect of this trip. Thus, it should come as no surprise that I wasn't exactly turning cartwheels when my dad decided that it was high time we loaded up the family station wagon and make a pilgrimage to our family's fabled homeland of Breaux Bridge, Louisiana. With a chip on my shoulder and the typical teenage bad attitude, I hopped in the back seat with my sister and archenemy, Katie (as Dad would say, "we make Cain and Abel look like they got along good"). For hour upon hour I suffered through repeated listenings of all my parents' favorite songs, as well as my dad's stubborn insistence that he knew where we were going (which, of course, he didn't). I had it made up in my mind that I knew exactly what to expect from Breaux Bridge, Louisiana: a small town that looks nice on paintings and postcards but, up close and personal, is nothing more than a safe haven for mosquitoes.

Instead, what I got from Breaux Bridge was one of the greatest cultural experiences a person could ask for. Well hidden in the swamplands is a vibrant bunch of people who have truly stood the test of time. These are people who still say their prayers in French. These are the same people who still realize that the day is for work and the night is for good-natured fun. These are people who didn't forget where they came from—they brought it with them. They have their own language, dances, songs, and basic outlook on life. And, probably most importantly, they have a recipe for just about anything with a pulse. They are Cajuns, and they have much to be proud of.

Having originally come to the United States as refugees from Nova Scotia, the Cajun people know what it is like to have the carpet literally pulled out from under their feet. They had everything they could want in Nova Scotia but were basically forced out by English occupation. The move from Canada was difficult, but they survived—and so did their culture. This is not to say that their new lives were easy. In fact, many Cajuns were made to work long, hard hours for extremely low wages. Their lack of education made them easy to take advantage of, and many lost what little they did have to the natural disasters in their newfound home. And yet, somehow, through it all, the Cajun people have maintained an undying sense of youth and pride. They are not a broken people. They are very much alive and well, with the basic attitude of "smile, it could be a lot worse." In a lot of ways I guess my dad is the same way.

Growing up, my dad was always a bit different from most of his peers. I guess he was a bit of a loner, and believe me, loneliness is not the easiest thing to deal with. In his adolescent years, my dad spent most of his time working at the family auto parts store instead of going out and having good times with his friends. Surely this must have been hard on a teenage boy with an abundance of energy. And, of course, when my dad reached adulthood, he was diagnosed with multiple sclerosis, which is devastating for anyone to find out. And yet somehow, just like the Cajuns of Breaux Bridge, my dad has managed to keep his head up. I think that's the basic message, not just of Cajun humor, but of Cajun life in general: things aren't always going to be easy, but you may as well smile because, ultimately, everything will be all right. This is an extremely redeeming message in a world that seems all too ready to give up. We can all learn a lot from a Cajun. It's best to be happy.

This book is one of the many ways in which a Cajun can make you happy. It's set in Breaux Bridge, Louisiana, and as I have said before, the people there really are some crazy characters (some are too crazy to be put in the book!). I will honestly say that I do not regret the trip to Breaux Bridge, just as you will not regret going there yourself by reading this book. I'm not sure if there's a "moral to the story," but one thing is for sure: the heart of a Cajun will endure.

JASON

ACKNOWLEDGMENTS

The old saying "No man is an island" is very true, especially when it came to putting all of the stories my granpa tole me into this book. I'd like to thank: Ms. Denise McMullen Robare of Quicksilver Services, who spent countless hours at the typewriter making sure my stories came across on paper the best they could; Mr. Dominicus ("Don") Maters, an invaluable asset, sitting at his drawing board, drawing and redrawing all of the illustrations until they captured the full flavor of the stories and brought all of the characters to life; and my son, Jason, who not only wrote the foreword of this book but helped me word the introduction to help people comprehend my relationship with Granpa to the fullest.

Last but not least, I would like to thank all of the people at Pelican Publishing for giving me the opportunity to do the three things I dearly love: tell Cajun stories, make people laugh, and tell folks about my granpa and family.

INTRODUCTION

Hello dere, y'all, and welcome to my world of Cajun humor. It is a world where the number one rule is "be happy and forget about all the things that make you unhappy." Like everyone else, I have my fair share of worries here in the real world, namely: having multiple sclerosis, two children in college, and a head that used to be a member of "The Hair Lite Club" but now belongs to (as my friend Bob Mahoney refers to it) "The Hair Free Club." I also have to worry about being the husband my wife, Cathy, deserves; a brother to my sisters, Emilie and Anna; a good son to my parents, Helen and Emile; a good Uncle T. J. to my nephews, Michael Christian and Nicholas Emile (our newest 11 lb. 5 oz. family member born on August 26, 1997), and my nieces, Jessica Maria and Kathleen Marie; a good parrain (pronounced "pie ran," dat's Cajun for "godfather") to my nephew, Joseph Lawrence, and my niece, Madeleine Claire; and a good "Tom" for my three special little people, David V (we call him Quint; I'm his parrain too), his sister Anna, and Olivia (we call her Wivie G). Those three defy the old saying "Blood is thicker than water." I also have to be a good brother-in-law to my brothers-in-law, Tommy, Jimmy,

Darin, and Mike, and my sisters-in-law, Carmen and Jennifer. I also have my son-in-law duties: let my mother-in-law, Verne, and father-in-law, Harold (everyone calls him "Flash"), know that their daughter married someone who loves her dearly and will always be there for her. And of course, I have to be a good owner to my dog, Annie. Aside from the family, however, one of my biggest concerns is letting you, the reader, know exactly where I'm coming from with my humor.

For a lot of people, the term "Cajun humorist" means someone who makes fun of Cajun people. Let me tell you, *nothing* could be farther from the truth when it comes to my humor. My goal is not to ridicule but, rather, to preserve the Cajun culture with the dignity and respect it deserves. More specifically, I want to preserve the memory of my granpa, Gilbert.

I have two vivid memories of my granpa. When I was around 12 years old Granpa would bring me to his night-watching job at the City Barn, where all the city equipment (bulldozers, street sweepers, garbage trucks, etc.) was kept. I loved night watching with Granpa because it always started with a ride in the police car with officers Lemon Creel and Richard ("Big Wes") West. Granpa never drove, but being a city employee, he could always get a ride from the police. We would ride in the back of that police cruiser, and they would sound the siren for me and flash the lights, and that big shotgun between the two officers made me feel like a real big shot. Once the officers dropped us off at the City Barn, I would play on all of the equipment, watch Granpa knit castnets for fishermen, and listen to stories about the people, places, and things in and around Granpa's hometown (and homeland) of Breaux Bridge, Louisiana.

Granpa and his family were forced to leave Breaux Bridge thanks to the Great Mississippi River Flood of 1927. The farm that the family was sharecropping was destroyed in the flood, and they were forced to seek refuge in Biloxi, Mississippi, where the seafood factories were going strong and the only qualifications needed for a job were a will to work and a strong back. But let me assure you: *you can take the Cajun out of the bayou, but you can't take the bayou out of the Cajun.* In other words, just because Granpa crossed the state line, he did not lose his "Cajun-ness." Everything came with him and the family—their faith, language, heritage, cooking, and, most of all, their humor and good nature. All of this came across to me on those long nights when I would sit at Granpa's knee, mesmerized by his every word.

Things were great until around 1969 when Granpa's lung cancer, which had been in remission since 1964, reappeared. The treatment for cancer in those days was cobalt, which can best be described as being put into a microwave. On the days when Granpa went to the Veterans Administration for his treatments, I would be waiting for him back home with a lukewarm bath, drawn to cool his burned and blistered skin. Granpa could not walk after those treatments, so as a strong, 15-year-old boy, I would carry him from the car to the tub and then to bed. I would get him dressed into his pajamas (we always called them "pee-jays") and tuck him in for the evening.

My humor is all about the good times, knitting castnets, fishing, night watching, and laughing with Granpa. I choose to remember the good times because they don't hurt like those latter memories, but still I realize that you have to take the good with the bad (that's all you can do sometimes). My life with Granpa ended on October 2, 1970, but his memory will live on, thanks in part to readers like you who I hope will share these stories with all of your friends and loved ones. I love my granpa and I'm sure that as you read through the Cajun stories my granpa tole me you will come to love him, too.

CAJUN STORIES MY GRANPA TOLE ME

Wan some people tink 'bout a Cajun, dey tink 'bout somebody who can look at a rice field an' tell you how many gallons of gumbo it would take to cover it. Well, dat's right. Some people tink dat's dem people who don't talk like everybody else; well, dat's right too.

In reality, Cajun is de mutilation of de word Acadian. De Acadian were a group of people who moved out of France into Nova Scotia an' dere dey settles down an' averythin' was goin' 'long fine till one day de Queen Mama, over in England, took a notion dat she would like to have a little piece of property, namely Nova Scotia. Well folks, de king was like any odder husband, he didn't want to leave his wife's complaint compartment open too long, so he sent some people over to talk wit' dem Acadian people an' tell dem dey was gonna have to swear allegiance to de king an' queen of England.

Well, I gotta tole you dat didn't set good wit' dem Acadian people one little bitty bit an' dey didn't swear to de king an' queen of England, dey swear at em, an' real good, too. Dem Acadian folks all loaded up deir boats an' started down de East Coast of de United States. Some of dem settled in Virginia, some of dem settled in de Carolinas, some in Georgia, some in Florida, some of dem on de Gulf Coast of Alabama an' Mississippi, most of dem settled in South Louisiana, an' some of dem had some real good navigators on deir boats—dey wound up in Texas somewhere. But wit' dem early settlers dey brought dis tang we call Cajun Humor. It's a humor dat we laugh at ourseffs, averybody else, an' pass a good time.

So now dat you know me a little better, I guess it's time to get on wit' de stories an' pass a good time wit' all of y'all, so kick back, relax, an' get to readin' dem Cajun stories my granpa tole me.

CHAPTER 1
Elmo an' Marie

EMERGENCY

DIM LIGHTS

It's no secret to anyone who has listened to my tapes, seen my two videos, or read my first book, *Cajun Humor from the Heart,* dat my cuzin Elmo Breaux an' his wife, Marie, are always arguin' 'bout one tang or de odder. So, it came as no surprise to ole Skinny Chenet, who went to de Breaux Bridge Hospital to visit his fran, Amus Doucet (pronounced Dew Say), to see Marie pushin' a wheel chair wit' Elmo sittin' in it out de mergency room door. Ole Skinny look at Elmo an' he have on a neck brace, back brace, cast on both arm, cast on both leg (well, one an' a haf leg—y'all learn more 'bout dat in de next story), an' a whole bunch of stitches scattered all over de place.

Skinny look an' say, "Coo yi yi, Elmo, wat de worl' happen to you?"

Well, Elmo try to answer, but all he could did was mumble.

Skinny say, "Elmo, I'm sorry to have to made you talk again, but I can't undastood one word you say."

As usual, Marie had to took over de conversation an' did all de talkin' for Elmo. Marie look at Skinny an' said, "Skinny, Elmo's tryin' to tole you dat he finally got de answer to dat 'Why should I be de first one to dim my brite lights on de car?' question he's always axin'."

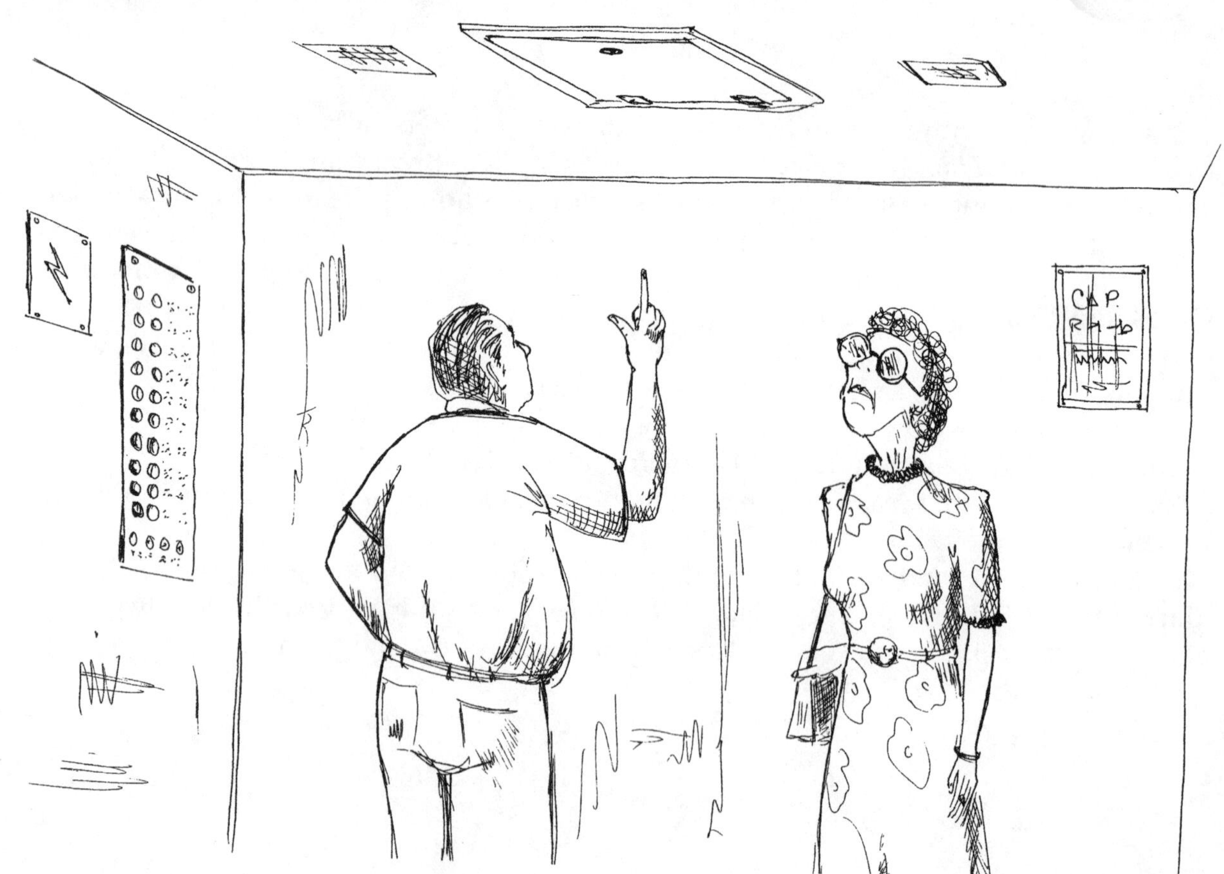

Brave Husband

My cuzin Elmo Breaux is well taught of in de Breaux Bridge area, mostly 'cause he's a real nice fella to talk wit'. Odder folks 'round Breaux Bridge respeck Elmo 'cause he is a war hero dat loss one of his leg in de war fightin' unda General McArceneaux (yeah, he was Cajun, but afta he made a name for hisseff he change his name to McArthur). Elmo gets 'long fine wit' averybody 'sept his wife, Marie. One day, Elmo an' Marie had to go over to Baton Rouge to took care of some business an' de office dey needed to go to for dat business was in one of dem tall buildin' 'bout 20 story high. So dey got on dat eluvator an' push de floor #18 button where dat office was at, an' won't you know dat eluvator came to a dead stop on de 15½ floor. Well, let me tole you, dem two don't got 'long in a 50-acre field much less in a 10 x 10 eluvator.

Afta 'bout 20 minute of yellin' an' screamin' for somebody to help an' gettin' no kind of answer, Elmo look at Marie an' say, "Marie, you know wat I'm taught?"

Marie say, "No, Elmo, I ain't no mine reader, wat you taught?"

Elmo say, lookin' up at dat little attic lookin' door hole in de ceilin' of de eluvator, "I'm taught somebody could go up true dat door hole dere an' get on top dis eluvator. Den dat somebody could grab hole of dem cable dat made dis tang go up an' down. Den dat somebody could slide down dat cable for dem 15½ floor to de first floor, pry de doors open, an' got some help."

Marie got all white in de face an' say, "Oh no, dat's way too dangerous to even taught 'bout Elmo. I wish you woulda nava tole me dat. I'm gonna be up all night broke out in de sweat jus' tinkin' 'bout dat. Why de worl' did you even brung dat up, Elmo, why, tell me why?"

Elmo got all red in de face an' he start yell, "Alrite, alrite Marie, dat's 'nuff, I don't wanna hear no more outa you, an' beside, I was jus' suggest dat, I ain't got no intention of makin' *you* do it!"

Regular Checkout an' Exercise

My cuzin Elmo an' his wife, Marie, have deir faults, but one tang dey got goin' for dem is dey both always go for a yearly checkout at Dr. Duplichan's office. One year afta deir checkout, Dr. Duplichan call dem in his office an' tole dem dey was both O.K. in de health department, but dey both was overweight an' needed to not only cut down on de gumbo, potato salad, an' jambalya, but add some regular exercise to dat diet to be successful.

'Bout two months later ole Dr. Duplichan see Elmo in town an' boy was he surprise to see Elmo done slim down to a lean, mean, Cajun machine. Dr. Duplichan say, "Coo yi yi, Elmo, you look good! I'm so proud dat you took my advise. Wat you been did to look so good?"

Elmo say, "Well, Doc, I took up golf an' whoo I love dat game. I play 18 hole averyday an' sometime 36 on Saturday an' Sunday."

Dr. Duplichan say, "Well, I'm gonna tole you dat you look real, real good. But wat 'bout Marie? How she did?"

Elmo say, "Well, Doc, I sure wish you woulda' nava ax me dat. Dat's a real sore subject 'round our house, I garontee."

Dr. Duplichan say, "Wat's wrong wit' Marie, Elmo?"

Elmo say, "Well, Doc, like I been tole you, I go golfin' averyday, but Marie ain't touched a one of dem exercise garden tools or lawnmower I got for her."

I'm
DROWNING
STUPID!

SCUBA CAJUN

In deir 25 years of marriage, Elmo an' Marie exchanged a whole bunch of birthday, anniversary, an' Christmas present, but nothin' in Elmo's book aver topped de present Marie gave him for his 40th Over-De-Hill birthday party. De big box from Marie contain a complete frogman outfit of undawater mask, tanks, flipper, wet suit—plus an undawater writin' tablet an' an undawater writin' pencil. Elmo grab up all dat stuff, true it in back his truck, an' head for Bayou Teche. Elmo slip into all dat 'quipment an' dove in headfirst. Elmo was swimmin' all 'round an' won't you know he run into his fran, Emile Robichaw. Elmo grab hold of dat undawater writin' tablet an' dat undawater writin' pencil an' wrote Emile a note dat said, "Marie spent a whole lot of money buyin' me dis frogman outfit to stay unda de water, but how could you stay unda 'cause you ain't got no 'quipment on at all?"

Emile grab dat undawater writin' tablet an' pencil out Elmo's hand, erase dat question, an' start wrote his own note dat said, "I'm not stayin' unda 'cause I want to, Elmo. *I'm drownin', Stupid!*"

De Begga Fella

One day my cuzin Elmo was walkin' in downtown Breaux Bridge an' he run into dis fella on de corner wit' his hat off beggin' him for a little loose pocket change. Elmo look at dat fella an' tole him, "Look, I done heard 'bout you kind planty time so I'm gonna ax you a question an' if you answer dat question honest I'll gave you five dollas. Is dat a deal?"

De fella say, "Oh yes, sir, for five dollas I'll answer any question you ax me honest as ole Abe Lincoln, I garontee."

Elmo say, "O.K. Are you gonna use dat money to go buy some whiskey?"

De begga fella say, "No, sir. I'm not a drinkin' man. My mama an' daddy raised me up to nava drank dat nasty tastin' stuff."

Elmo say, "Well, maybe you gonna use dat money to buy youseff some tobacco, cigarette, cigar, or a plug of chew, haah?"

De begga fella say, "No, sir. I tried dat tobacco stuff one time an' whoo, it made me sick as a dog an' I'll nava made dat mistake again."

Elmo say, "Well, maybe you gonna use dat money to go gamble an' play a little Bourré [pronounced Boo Ray, Cajun Poker] or bet on some football game, haah?"

De begga fella say, "Oh no, sir, five dollas won't get you into no Bourré game an', beside dat, I ain't nava had no interest in any kind of gamblin'. I need dat money to go buy myseff somethin' to eat. I'm tired, cold, an' hungry, my fran."

Elmo snatch up dat begga fella an' march him rite down to his house, into his livin' room. Marie was in de kitchen fixin' supper wan she heard Elmo callin' her at de top of his lung, from de livin' room, "Marie, come see wat I got rite now! Marie, come here fass as you can!"

Marie come runnin' in de livin' room only to see Elmo standin' dere wit' dat poor ole run-down begga fella dat needed a bath an' a shave real bad, not to mention new clothes 'cause de ones he have on was full of holes. Marie call Elmo off to de side an' ax him, "Why de worl' did you brung dat poor ole fella home an' not down to one of dem shelter place?"

Elmo say, "Oh dat's de next stop we gonna make, but I wanted you to see firsthand wat happens to a man wan he don't drink, smoke, or gamble so you won't be fussin' at me no more!"

CHAPTER 2
T'Bub's

50
20

Birthday Suit

De folks who have read my first book, *Cajun Humor from the Heart*, or listened to any of my six cassettes, or watched my videos, know de numba-one hungout in Breaux Bridge, Louisiana, for my granpa an' his frans was T'Bub's Barroom. It was a place where men could talk 'bout fishin', huntin', sports, an' women, an' averybody was interested an' agreed wit' wat was say, 'specially 'bout women. Some of my favorite stories Granpa tole me as a kid came out of T'Bub's an', by far, de one 'bout old Amos Bordelon goin' to one of dem nudist camps is one of my favorites.

Granpa tole me Amos got back from his nudist camp trip an' naturally he had averybody's full attention an' center stage to tell dem all 'bout de camp. Amos say, "Well, befo I got start tole y'all 'bout dat camp, I wanna got one tang clear—it ain't all it's crack up to be, I could garontee you dat."

Averybody say, "Wat you mean by dat, Amos?"

Amos say, "Well, to tole y'all de trueff, it's kinda' embarrassin'."

Averybody say, "Wat's de matter, Amos, you ashame of you birthday suit?"

Amos say, "No, I'm not ashame of my birthday suit at all, I'm jus' sayin' it's hard to look you bess wan you walkin' 'round wit' you pocket change an' you wallet in you mouth all de time."

Pie R Square

I always loved to hear my granpa talk 'bout de day wan ole T'New Pratt come walkin' in T'Bub's wit' his chess all puff up, wit' his arm 'round his boy, T'New Jr., wat had come home for spring broke from LSU College. Ole T'New was talkin' loud an' proud 'bout T'New Jr. did dis at LSU . . . an' T'New Jr. did dat at LSU . . . wan finally averybody say, "T'New, let Jr. talk for hisseff."

T'New Sr. look at T'New Jr. an' say, "Boy, pass some of dat LSU College talk on all dese fellas here."

Li'l' T'New Jr. look at dem an' say, "Pie R Square."

Whoo yi yi, wan Jr. got dat out his mouth, dare was T'New Sr., all red in de face, an' all a sudden he grab T'New Jr. by de troat an' drug him into de men's room. Big T'New say, "Boy, dat education taught you to sass an' make a fool out you daddy like dat?"

Li'l' T'New say wit' his voice all crack up from his daddy's grip on his throat, "Wat de worl' you talkin' 'bout, Daddy?"

T'New Sr. say, "Dat Pie R Square you jus' tole averybody. Me an' you maw don't got no education at all, but we got 'nuff sense to know brick are square, pie are round."

De Smuggler

One of de fellas dat hung 'round T'Bub's was named Ollie Ollier (pronounced Ole Yea) but averybody call him B. G. 'cause he was a retired Border Guard who was born an' raise in Breaux Bridge, but his job forced him to move to Brownsville, Texas guardin' de border for 25 years. Afta B. G. had put in his time, de magnetism of Breaux Bridge brought him back to his homeland. B. G. did return wit' one dark cloud hangin' over him an' dat was to have nava caught dis suspicious-lookin' character named Ace dat went back an' forth cross de border, true his station, for years. De first time B. G. laid his eye on Ace he knew he was guilty of smugglin' somethin' so he axed Ace, "Wat you got in de trunk of dis car?"

Ace say, "I got some bags."

B. G. say, "Wat's in dem bags?"

Ace say, "Dirt."

B. G. say, "I don't believe dat, pull over." So one by one B. G. went true avery bag in dat trunk. He aven have de dogs come sniff de dirt to try an' fine sometang illegal, but he nava came up wit' nothin'.

For years, de war between Ace an' B. G. continued. Avery car Ace drove true, B. G. tore apart an' nava came up wit' nothin' illegal. Well, low an' behold, B. G. was in T'Bub's wan in walks dat Ace character. B. G. watched him for a while, den finally walked over to de bar an' stood rite next to Ace, tapped him on de shoulder, an' axed him, "Hey, Ace, you remember me?"

Ace say, "Yeah, B. G., I rememba you, wat's goin' on?"

B. G. say, "Well, I retired from my Border Guard job an' moved back here to my hometown an' homeland, Breaux Bridge, Louisiana. How 'bout you?"

Ace say, "Well, like you, I'm retired too."

B. G. say, "Well, Ace, now dat we both retire an' I can't did a tang in de worl' to you now, answer me one question."

Ace say, "O.K. If I can, I'll answer dat question."

B. G. say, "O.K. For 25 years you passed true my guard station, an' I tore averytang apart, on avery car you drove true de station in, tryin' to catch you smugglin' sometang an' I know you was guilty, so don't lie, was I rite an' wat de worl' was you smugglin'?"

Ace say, "Yeah, B. G., you was rite . . . an' I was smugglin' cars."

De Loser

De crew at T'Bub's was a second family to most of de fellas dat hung out dare an' a first family to a few. De close-knit group had deir fair share of ups an' downs, but wan it came down to de nitty gritty, dey all stuck together like glue. One of de fellas who was a member of de group was ole Loser Lançon (pronounced Lawn Son), who had nava won a tang in his life. De crew got together an' started plannin' to made ole Loser a winner for de first time in his life. De plan was to sell raffle tickets for a pirogue (pronounced pee-row, a Cajun canoe) dat some of de fellas got together an' fixed up. All de raffle tickets had de same numba on dem, dat numba was 10.

As usual, ole Loser bought a ticket an' even commented, "I'll buy one, but I nava win anytang, I'm jus' wastin' my money."

De big day came wan de winnin' ticket was bein' drawn out, wit' averyone in agreement dat wan 10 was called nobody would claim it an' ole Loser would finally win for de first time in his life. All de tickets were put in a hat an' averybody say, "Loser, you draw de numba out de hat."

Loser reached in de hat sayin', "Somebody lucky is fixin' to have a nice pirogue to go fishin' in, I know it's not me."

After he pull de numba out de hat, averybody was grinnin' ear to ear an' say, "O.K., Loser, wat's de numba?"

Loser look at it an' say, "6¾."

200 LBS
BARBELL SET DELUXE
US MAIL
US MAIL
300 LBS

Mail Order Weight Set

In today's worl', we have spas an' fitness centers full of all kinds of exercise machines an' equipment to help shape our bodies into lean, fat-free works of art. In my granpa's day, dey had hard work or simply a set of bar bell, like Granpa call dem. I often tink 'bout ole Knute Guidry wan I see one of dese fitness centers an' recall de story Granpa tole me 'bout de time Knute was in T'Bub's an' tole averybody he was lookin' in de mail order Sears an' Sawbuck catalog an' order hisseff one of dem bar bell set.

Averybody say, "De whole set? Coo yi yi, dat set you back some money, huh?"

Knute say, "Well, not de way I'm buyin' it. I'm on dis special plan dat let you buy one piece at de time so you don't got to buy de whole set at one crack. Avery odder day or so dey mail me a new piece."

Averybody say, "Well, Knute, dat sound like a good deal, but you don't look no different since you start work out."

Knute say, "Well, dat's 'cause I'm waitin' to get de whole set together at one time, but I hope wan I start I could look jus' haf as good as my mailman does since he start brung me all dem barbell pieces."

BOSS
OF THE
KITCHE

Be de Man

Jus' like I tole y'all at de start of dis chapter, T'Bub's Barroom is de numba-one hungout in Breaux Bridge ware men could talk 'bout fishin', huntin', sports, an' women. It's a place ware averybody was interested an' agreed wit' wat was say, 'specially 'bout women. Well, one day de conversation got 'round to bein' de man of de family, an' whoo yi yi, ole Dig Fontenot (pronounced Font In No)—dey call him Dig 'cause he was a backhoe operator—went off like one of dem Roman candle. Dig say, "Let me tole y'all who wares de pants in my family. Jus' lass nite we run out of hot water an' I start raise 14 kind of heck, an' I garontee you my wife was on de phone callin' up de hot water fella an' in jus' a hour dat problem got fix an' I have de hot water runnin'."

Averybody in T'Bub's start clappin' an' whistlin' an sayin', "Alrite, Dig! Dat's de way to go! Be *de man*, whoo yeah, Dig, you de man of you house, we garontee you dat."

Dig fanish, took his bows, an' turn 'round to face de bar ware T'Bub have him a bottle of beer on de house waitin' for him. Dig took a big swallow, den he look at T'Bub an' unda his breath he mumble, "You know, T'Bub, it jus' ain't fair for a woman to make a man wash dishes in cold water is it?"

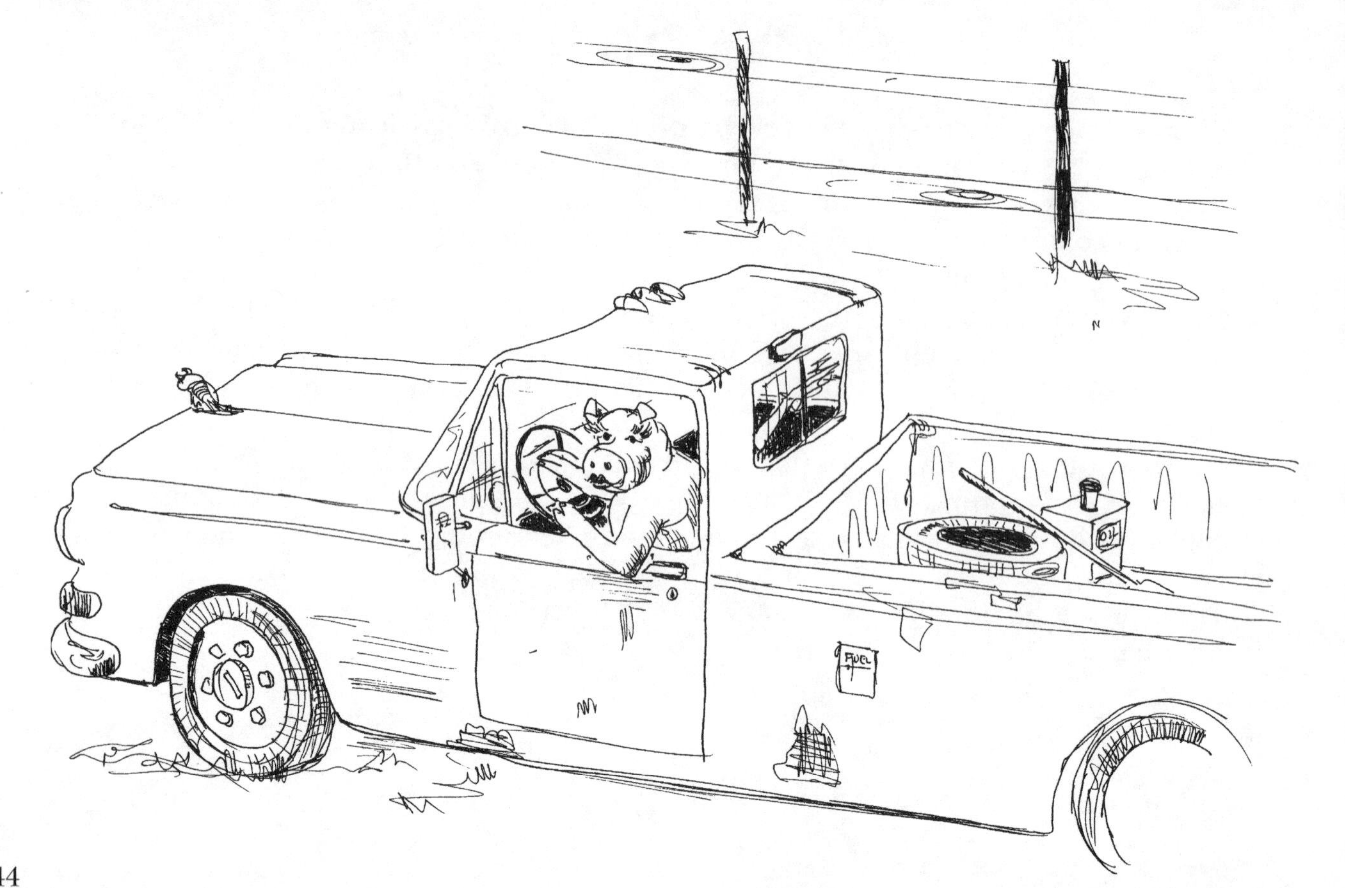
OIL
FUEL

Breed dat Sow

T'Bub's was a place ware many deals were made, fishin' stories tole, an' sports events talked 'bout. De deal made between Emmitt Le Blanc an' Emile Fontenot is by far de one I loved to hear my granpa tell over an' over again.

De story goes, Emmitt had a beautiful blue-ribbon-prizewinnin' sow dat averybody kept tole him to breed an' kep de bloodline goin'. It was in T'Bub's dat Emmitt met Emile Fontenot, who tole him he jus' happen to have a blue-ribbon-prize boar at his house. Afta some drankin' an' talkin' dem two fellas decide to got dem pigs together. De nex mornin', Emmitt load up dat sow in de back his truck an' drove her down to Fontenot's farm.

Dat evenin', wan he got off work he stop by Fontenot's to pick up his sow an' ax Fontenot, "How I'm gonna know if dat took?"

Fontenot say, "Well, in de mornin' if you see her rollin' in de mud dat mean it don't took, but if she's layin' out in de sun dat means it took, an' good too."

Well, de nex mornin', Emmitt run to look out de kitchen window dat face de barnyard an' dere was dat sow rollin' all 'round in de mud. Emmitt load up dat sow in de back his truck again an' drop her off at Fontenot's house on de way to work. Dat evenin' he go pick her up again an' de nex mornin' wan Emmitt look out dat kitchen window de news was de same as de day befo, de sow was rollin' in de mud again. Emmitt load her back up an' went true all dat bringin' an' pickin' up again.

De nex mornin', Emmitt tole his wife, Kitty, "Please go look out de window. My eyes can't stood no more disappointment like I been seein' de lass few days."

Well, Kitty go look out dat kitchen window an' don't say a word.

Emmitt say, "Well, I guess you don't wanna be de one to brokes de bad news. She rollin' in de mud again, huh?"

Kitty say, "No, Emmitt, she ain't did dat."

Whoo, ole Emmitt got all excite. "You mean to tole me it took an' she's layin' in de sun?"

Kitty say, "No, she ain't did dat neither, Emmitt."

Emmitt say, "Well, if she ain't roll in de mud or lay in de sun, wat's she did?"

Kitty say, "She's in de front seat of you truck, blowin' de horn. She ready to go."

Close Family

T'Bub's was a home away from home for many of Breaux Bridge residents an' a lot of news, good an' bad, was talked 'bout in T'Bub's 'cause T'Bub was always dere, like any good bartanda, to lend an' ear to his customers (I believe T'Bub had a streak of nosey in him, too). One day, ole T'Boy Savoy was downin' dem drank one afta de odder an' T'Bub say, "T'Boy, it ain't none of my business, but why de worl' you drank like dat? I ain't nava know you to drank like dat!"

T'Boy say, "Well, T'Bub, I gots some bad, bad news today."

T'Bub say, "Wat bad news could made you drank like dat, T'Boy?"

T'Boy say, "I got lay off at my job, is dat bad 'nuff for you, T'Bub?"

T'Bub say, "Yeah, dat's some bad news alrite, but you gots to look at de brite side wan tangs like dat happen."

T'Boy say, "Wat could be de brite side of sometang like dat, T'Bub?"

T'Bub say, "Well, it ain't been six month ago ole Alex Hebert [pronounced A Bear] got lay off at his job an' he tole me dat his gettin' fired at his job brung his family closer together dan it had aver been in a whole lot of year."

T'Boy say, "Why you magine dat happen, T'Bub? Could it be dat dem hard time made averybody have to join' forces an' pull together to made ends meet?"

T'Bub say, "Well, I guess dat was part de reason too, but I tink de main reason was Alex have to sell his big 10-room house an' move into a li'l bitty 3-room 'partment."

Hair Tonic

It's hard to be a good sport wan de joke's on you, but I try to hung in dere wan somebody starts pickin' on ball-headed men 'cause I'm one of dem troops, or like my fran Bob Mahoney refers to us, De Hair Free Generation. I like dat.

De one story dat comes to mind is de time ole Cue Saucier (pronounced So Shea) was in T'Bub's an' informed averybody, "Y'all gonna be callin' me H. Cue pretty soon, I garontee y'all dat."

Averybody axed, "Wat de worl' does dat stan for, Cue?"

Cue say, "Dat stan for 'Hairy Cueball,' y'all."

Averybody say, "How de worl' you figure dat?"

Cue say, "Well, I was down at Clair Réaux's [pronounced Ray Oh] barber shop an' while Clair was trimmin' up my monk ring he start tole me afta 50 year of bein' a barber, he done brew up a tonic dat will grow hair on a cueball an' dat he wanna gave me a bottle to prove his brew really works. Clair tole me I have to work in dat brew real hard wit' my fingers two time a day an' I was gonna see planty hair real soon."

Averybody say, "Well, Cue, how long you been did dat?"

Cue say, "Well, I'm goin' on 'bout eight week now."

Averybody in T'Bub's say, "Eight week? We don't see no hair or even peachfuzz on you head, Cue."

Cue say, "Well, jus' gave it some time to caught on up dere on my head. I'm already havin' to shave my fingers twice a day."

Double Xs

Granpa tole me T'Bub's was a place dat de bull got mighty tick an' deep, too. It was also de place ware if you had sometang to sell like a boat, motor, or huntin' tangs like guns, deer stans, or campin' supplies you could almost be sure to fine a buyer. I wanna focus in on one of dem deals between Snuff Guidry an' Mutt Barrio. It seem dat Snuff got hisseff a bran-spankin'-new shotgun for his birthday an' he was tryin' to sell his ole shotgun to buy de case an' odder tangs for his new gun wat he jus' got.

Well, it jus' so happen dat Mutt Barrio was in de market for a new shotgun an' de deal Snuff was offerin' was jus' too good to pass up, so ole Mutt say, "Write me up de bill of sale an' you done sole youseff a gun, my fran."

Snuff tole Mutt, "My hand is hurtin' bad wit' dat ole arthur [meanin' arthritis]. You wrote dat bill out an' I'll pass a sign [signature] on it."

Ole Mutt grab some paper an' wrote out all de "he sole de gun, I bought de gun" information on dere an' den he pass dat paper over to Snuff an' say, "Sign 'em rite dere."

Snuff took de pancil an' wrote, "Xx."

Mutt den realize dat arthur was jus' an' excuse dat Snuff gave him 'cause he couldn't read or write, so he don't say a word 'sept, "Snuff, wat's dat little 'x' for?"

Snuff say, "Well, Mutt, I don't want dat paper to get mess up wit' my daddy 'cause I'm a junior."

De Big Star

I guess de biggest name dat aver pass true T'Bub's was Elvis Premeaux (pronounced Pre Moe)—Presley afta he got rich an' famous. Elvis was down 'round Breaux Bridge, did a movie, an' de director brung him into T'Bub's to talk, "loosen him up," 'bout de lass scene he was tinkin' 'bout for de movie dey was makin'.

De director say, "Elvis, you rememba dat high cliff we was stood on today overlookin' dat place call Little Bayou?"

Elvis say, "Yeah, I rememba dat."

De director say, "Well, I'm taught 'bout havin' you dive off dat cliff into dat bayou an' rescue de girl, how's dat sound?"

Elvis say, "Dat sounds like you crazy, my fran. Dat cliff was 'bout 200 feet high an' dat bayou is 'bout 11 inches deep an' full of snakes, gators, an' lord knows wat else."

De director order dem up two of T'Bub's famous B52 dranks ('cause afta one you feel like somebody drop a bomb on you) an' jus' as Elvis was drank down de lass few drop, dat director look at him rite in de eyes an' say, "Now, Elvis, do you taught for one minute we would let a big star like you drown?"

CHAPTER 3
Coo Coo Comeaux

Loose Noose

T'Bub's was always packed, 'specially in de evenin' afta averybody got off work, an' on de weekend, ha, sardines ain't packed dat tite, I garontee. A place like T'Bub's always seem to have dat one customer averybody loves to pick on an' talk 'bout an' you could be for sure dat customer at T'Bub's was a fella named Coo Coo Comeaux (pronounced Ko Moe). Coo Coo was one of dem people us Cajuns call "ain't correct," but dat run in de poor boy's family.

My granpa tole me dat Coo Coo's great-granpa was caught robbin' crabtraps out in de bayou wit' dese odder two fellas, an' back in dem days Granpa say, "Folks took matters into deir own hand to save de police all de trouble." Well, it jus' so happened de crab-traps dey was robbin' belong to ole Scar Thibodaux an' his boys (Scar got dat nickname from not only all de scars he got from fightin', but de ones on his hands ware he would empty de traps bare hand an' nava flinch wan one of dem big blue claws grabbed hold of one of his fingers). Scar an' his boy decide to hung Coo Coo's great-granpa an' dem odder two fellas rite on de spot, so dey grab de rope in dere, trowed it over one of dem big limbs on de nearest cypress tree, wrap it 'round dat first fella's neck, an' let him drop.

De fella's luck was wit' him dat day, 'cause de rope slip off his neck over his head, an' let me tole y'all, Granpa say, "Ole Johnny Wisemellon woulda been proud of how fass dat crabtrap robber swim off." Scar an' his boys grab de second theif an', won't you know, de same tang happen, an' he could swim faster dan de first fella.

Scar an' his boys was gettin' real mad by dis time an' dey grab up ole Coo Coo's great-granpa an' dey look at him an' say, "We gonna did de job rite dis time, fella, we garontee you dat."

Coo Coo's great-granpa look at dem an' say, "Well, I sure hope so y'all, 'cause I can't swim a lick."

Fur ala Coo Coo

Wit' a family tree like his great-granpa in de Loose Noose story, ole Coo Coo Comeaux didn't have much of a chance to have an impact on de scholastic worl'. I guess de story I loved to hear my granpa tell 'bout ole Coo Coo de most was wan he come walkin' into de funeral home dress up in white fur from head to toe an' black shoe polish paint all over his nose. De funeral director, ole Guy B. Robear, took one look at dat an', coo yi yi, he run over to Coo Coo an' axed him why de worl' was he dress up like dat in his funeral home. Coo Coo say, "Well Guy B., y'all got my fran, ole J. B. Blanchard lay out here, huh?"

Guy B. say, "Yeah, we got J. B. Why you ax me dat?"

Coo Coo say, "Well, lass night his wife call an' tole me dat J. B. taught of me as one of his bess frans an' she wanted me to be one of de polar bears for his funeral."

Coo Coo's Skulls

I saved dis story 'bout T'Bub's till now, 'cause I wanted to gave y'all a full dose of Coo Coo Comeaux all at de same time. Granpa tole me one day a bunch of folk was sittin' 'round T'Bub's wan, low an' behold, in walks Coo Coo wit' de skull of a grown-up unda one arm an' de skull of a baby unda de odder. Granpa say, "Well, Coo Coo not only stop all de talkin' goin' on, but he busted up some of T'Bub's glasses wan folks dropped dem out deir hands afta seein' wat he was carryin'."

T'Bub finally broke de silence an' axed Coo Coo, "Wat de worl' you mean carryin' two skulls in my place dere?"

Coo Coo say, "Y'all ain't jus' lookin' at skulls, y'all lookin' at history."

Everybody say, "Wat you mean by dat?"

Coo Coo say, "Dat big one dere is de skull of none odder dan Jean Lafitte, de mos famous pirate in de history of Louisiana, an' I talked de fella wat owned it down to only one tousand dollars."

Everybody say, "Well, wat 'bout dat li'l one? Who dat is?"

Coo Coo say, "Well now, dat one not only took some tall talkin', but all de wheelin' an' dealin' I know to got dat one for only five hundred dollars."

Everybody say, "Well, Coo Coo, don't kep it a secret, who dat li'l one belong to?"

Coo Coo say, "Dat, my fran, is none odder dan Jean Lafitte wan he was a baby."

Who Kill Abe?

If you had de chance to read my first book, *Cajun Humor from the Heart,* I introduced you to de numba-one lawman in Breaux Bridge, Louisiana, Sheriff C'Ta Premeaux (pronounced Pre Moe). Well, Granpa tole me dat Sheriff C'Ta was in bad need of a new deputy an' three fellas showed up to interview for de job: René Broussard, Anizette Landry, an' yeah, Coo Coo Comeaux. C'Ta decide to gave dem all a fair chance; he would gave dem all a tess, so one at a time he brung dem into his office. De first one was René Broussard. Sheriff C'Ta look at René an' axed him, "Who kill Abe Lincoln?"

René say, "Well, John Wilkes Boof."

C'Ta say, "O.K., René, dat's all." Den he go get Anizette Landry, brung him into his office, an' axed him de same question, "Who kill Abe Lincoln?"

Anizette say, "Well, John Wilkes Boof."

C'Ta say, "O.K., Anizette, dat all." Den he go get Coo Coo sittin' out in de waitin' room, brung him into his office, an' axed him de same question, "Who kill Abe Lincoln?"

Boy, ole Coo Coo start scratch his head, cleared his troat, an' say, "C'Ta, do you mine if I gave dat some taught over de weekend?"

C'Ta say, "No, dat's fine wit' me."

Ole Coo Coo got home an' his wife, Dew, met him at de door all anxious an' axed him, "Did C'Ta like you, an' is he gonna gave you dat job?"

Coo Coo's chess got all swole up an' he say, "Did C'Ta like me? Cher, he's already got me workin' on a murder case."

SPANISH LESSONS

Granpa tole me a lot of stories 'bout ole Coo Coo Comeaux, but dis one is my favorite. Ole Coo Coo pass by ole Benny Fourniers (pronounced Foon Yeah) grocery store an' restaurant, dat's de place averybody hung out wan T'Bub's was closed, an' Benny axed Coo Coo, "Ware de worl' you been? I ain't seen you or you wife, Dew, in a coon's age."

Coo Coo say, "Well, Benny, I guess dat's 'cause Dew an' me been took some Spanish lesson at de nite school."

Benny say, "Spanish lesson! Why de worl' you been took dat?"

Coo Coo say, "Well, Benny, me an' Dew been try to have some children for a long time an' tangs jus' don't seem to be work out for us. We done made all de 'rangement to adopt a li'l baby."

Benny say, "Well, Coo Coo, dat's nice but dat still don't answer my question. Why dem Spanish lesson?"

Coo Coo say, "Well, Benny, it look like we gonna be gettin' a li'l Spanish baby, an' me an' Dew both wanna be able to undastand de baby wan it starts talkin'."

Coo Coo's Mama

De ole sayin' "Only a mother could love it" goes 'long wit' ole Coo Coo in spite of his lack of academic excellence. Granpa tole me one time Coo Coo's mama was in de beauty parlor an' she was sit rite between dese two women unda de hair dryers dat was braggin' 'bout deir kids. Wit' all dat air blowin', dey was talkin' way louder dan normal an' averbody in de beauty parlor, includin' Coo Coo's mama, could hear plain as day wat dey was sayin' 'bout deir children. One of dem lady say, "We so proud of our son, he is jus' 'bout to got out de medicine school an' he's gonna be a betta doctor dan Doc Duplichan." (I'll tell y'all 'bout him in de nex chapter.)

De odder lady say, "Well, our boy ain't as ole as you boy, but we jus' got de news from de school he was gonna be de valedictorian [or valet man, like Granpa use to say] of his class."

Well, poor ole Coo Coo's mama, who done have her an' ear an' belly full of dem two women, jump up an' say, "Well, let me tole you two ole bitties one tang. My boy Coo Coo was so excite wan he pass to de fifth grade, he cut his troat shavin'."

CHAPTER 4
Doc Duplichan

DUPLICHAN M.D.

De $50 Visit

When folks 'round Breaux Bridge got sick dere was no decision of ware dey was headed; it was off to Doc Duplichan's office. Granpa tole me ole Doc got some competition wan Emile Robichaw's (pronounced Robe A Shaw) boy got out de medicine school an' hung his shingle in Breaux Bridge, rite 'round de corner from ole Doc Duplichans's office.

Well, Granpa tole me dat news was buzzin' all 'round Breaux Bridge an' dese two women, Sadie Savoy an' Lena LeBlanc, was talkin'. Sadie tole Lena dat she was feelin' bad an' felt sorry for ole Emile's boy, 'cause he didn't have nobody goin' to him, so she went by to let him treat her. Sadie went on to say, "You know, Lena, Emile's boy only charge $10 a visit."

Lena say, "$10? Sadie, Doc Duplichan only charge $8."

Sadie say, "Well, Lena, I know dat, but de lass time I went to Doc Duplichan I had a cut on my finger dat only need two stitch. Well, Doc Duplichan put in dem two stitch, den he tole me we gotta took some ash trays [x-rays] to made for sure dere wasn't anytang broke. Well, I know I don't got no broke bone, but I let him check it out anyhow. An', Lena, won't you know dat befo I got out de office I done spand $50."

Lena say, "$50! On wat?"

Sadie say, "Well, ole Doc Duplichan talk me into buyin' two 8x10, three 5x7, an' twenty-four wallet-size pictures of dem ash trays."

T. PRATT
MISS EXPLORE SURGERY

De Unnecessary Operation

I guess y'all done figure out by now ole Doc Duplichan was a good doctor, but if he could squeeze a few extra dollars out of you, he would do it in a heartbeat, I garontee. Granpa tole me 'bout de time ole T'Pratt go for his regular checkout to Doc Duplichan, an' ole Doc start listen real close to his chess. Afta he fanish Doc say, "T'Pratt, I got some bad news to pass on you, my fran."

T'Pratt say, "Wat is it, Doc?"

Doc say, "Well, I don't like de sound of you chess, an' I believe we gonna have to did one of dem explore surgery on you."

T'Pratt say, "Hole on dere, Doc. I done have dat explore surgery year befo lass wan I come for my checkout. Den lass year you open me up again' afta my checkout, an' both time I didn't feel bad, an' both time you don't fine one tang wrong." T'Pratt say, "Doc, you now wat I taught?"

Doc Duplichan say, "No, T'Pratt, wat you taught?"

T'Pratt say, "I taught you been did all dat surgery on me an' some odder folk 'round here dat ain't necessary, but you did it anyhow jus' for de money, dat's wat I taught."

Doc Duplichan say, "Well, T'Pratt, you wanna know wat I taught?"

T'Pratt say, "You doggone rite I wanna know wat you taught!"

Doc Duplichan say, "I taught if I have to did it all over again I woulda nava named de yacht afta you, I garontee."

De Nurse

Ole Doc Duplichan was de man responsible for brought over half de folk in Breaux Bridge into de worl', but his nurse, Verna Lançon (pronounced Lawn Son), was at Doc's mama side wan he was born, so she had some kinda knowledge 'bout medicine an' helpin' patients in deir time of need. Granpa tole me 'bout de time ole A. J. Petijean (pronounced Pet A John) was in de hospital havin' all kinda tess run on him, an' wan Doc Duplichan was made his 'round at de hospital, Verna was alway rite dere beside him. Ole Doc went to A. J.'s room an' gave him all de result dem tess showed, but he tole him in all dat fancy doctor talk, an' A. J. don't undastood one word, so he axed Verna to stay a minute, he need to ax her somethin'. Doc say, "O.K., Verna, you talk wit' A. J. I'm goin' two door down. Come met me dere." An' den he leff de room.

Verna say, "O.K., A. J., wat you need to ax me?"

A. J. say, "Verna, I didn't undastood one word de doc tole me. Could you please tell me in plain English wat he say?"

Verna say, "A. J., I been a nurse for almost 60 year an' dere's one tang I know. If I tole you anytang 'bout dem tess I can't be a nurse no more, an' I don't wanna lose my job, 'specially afta all dem year."

A. J. say, "Well, Verna, I could respeck dat, but if you can't tell me 'bout dem tess, maybe you could got me a magazine or paper to read."

Verna say, "Oh, A. J., I'll be glad to did dat for you, an' I'm glad you only axed for a magazine or newspaper, 'cause you would nava live long 'nuff to read a book, I garontee."

LIVER PILLS

If dere's one tang my granpa believed in almost as much as de good Lord it was liver pills. In fack, he took his liver pill avery day an', wan I was wit' him, I had to swollow one down, too. I was always thankful dey figured out a way to put dat liver in a li'l pill, 'cause de taught of havin' to eat a big piece of dat liver sure sent chills up my twelve-year-ole back. I tink Granpa got de idea it was important to take dat liver medicine averyday from one of Doc Duplichan's patient, whose name was TooPee Touchet (pronounced Two Shea). I heard dis story jus' 'bout averytime I have to swollow dat liver pill down an' I wanna share it wit' y'all.

It seem dat TooPee took one of dem liver pill averyday, an' wan he was 90 year ole an' gettin' 'round like a spring chicken, averybody would always ax him, "How de worl' could you be 90 an' gettin' 'round like you do?"

TooPee would always answer, "Took care of you liver like I do an' you gonna live to tell people how you got so ole, too."

Well, Granpa say, "Dat TooPee finally pass away wan he was 101, but rumor had it dat afta tree days ole Doc Duplichan had to finally shoot his liver."

TO
SURGER
STAT

Speedy Cajun

I'm gonna let all you sport fans in on a li'l secret don't many people know 'bout but, tanks to my granpa, I can pass dis information on to all my frans. De fassest man in de worl' was a fella named Pal Barras. It seems dat Pal not only ran one mile in two minutes, but he did it rite out of his hospital bed in de expensive care unit in de Breaux Bridge hospital. "How?" y'all ax—well, here is de way it happen.

Doc Duplican was de numba-one doc 'round Breaux Bridge till li'l Emile Robichaw got out de medicine school an' went into computition wit' ole Doc Duplichan. Li'l Emile start notice wan he made his 'round at de hospital dat Doc Duplichan was doin' four to five operation avery day, an' he didn't believe all dem folk could need dat surgery. Well, li'l Emile was did his 'round in de expensive care unit wan he notice ole Pal Barras listen to de baseball game on de radio, cheerin' on his team, but at de same time he notice dis tag hung at de end of Pal's bed dat say "to surgery *stat*" (dat means *rite now*). Well, from wat li'l Emile saw, Pal needed a shave, but not surgery by a long shot. Li'l Emile go over to Pal's stall an' start talkin' wit' him an' doin' a complete checkout on Pal, head to toe.

Well, jus' 'bout dat time, Doc Duplichan come by an' seen li'l Emile checkin' out Pal. He walk over an' axed li'l Emile, "Wat you did wit' my patient, Pal, here?"

Li'l Emile say, "Well, Doc Duplichan, I been notice all dem operation you been did on all you patient, an' I believe half of dem ain't necessary."

Doc Duplichan say, "Well, dat's ware you wrong, boy, an' I don't appreciate you say dat."

Li'l Emile come rite back at him an' say, "Doc, I know you wrong, an' I'm gonna report you to de medicine board for did all dem unnecessary operation on people like ole Pal here."

Doc Duplichan say, "Don't talk to me like dat. Pal here need de operation I'm fixin' to did on him bad."

Li'l Emile say, "Oh no, Pal here don't need no operation."

So, dere dey was, one on each side de bed yellin' an' screamin' at each odder, "yeah he does, no he don't," wit' ole Pal Barras rite in de middle of dem, took in all dat fussin', movin' only his eyeballs back an' forth between dem two doctors.

Well, li'l Doc Robichaw finally say, "Doc Duplichan, I'm gonna leave now, but I'm comin' back an' I'm gonna have de medicine board folks wit' me."

De next words out Doc Duplichan's mouth were jus' like de gun goin' off to start Pal Barras's record-breakin' run. Doc Duplican say, "Well, brung dem medicine board folks wit' you 'round 3 P.M. an' I'm gonna prove I'm rite 'bout ole Pal here wan I did de autopsy."

Folks, for all I know, Pal is still runnin'.

CHAPTER 5
De Shrink

De Wrong Crop

Ole Doc Duplichan was de man for wat ached in you body, but wan it came to dealin' wit' problems in de head, Doc Troyhorn was de man to see. Granpa tole me dat Doc Troyhorn use to go over to T'Bub's an', avery once in a while, he would tell dem all 'bout one of his case dat was special. Granpa say, "Dat Doc Troyhorn always stay professional an' nava did use de name of his patient, he jus' tole dem wat J. C. Blanchard or E. B. Meaux had wrong wit' dem."

Granpa tole me, "De bess case I aver hear Doc Troyhorn talk 'bout in T'Bub's was wan he was sittin' at his desk did some paperwork, an' in walked dis fella wit' tomato plant stuck out both his ear, an' de vines hung down to his kneecaps, full of tomatoes."

Doc Troyhorn tole averybody, "Dat really startle me bad an' I went, 'Coo yi yi, wat de worl' is dat hung out you ears? Whew, dat's a first for me.'"

Doc Troyhorn tole averybody dat afta he blurt dat out he realize he don't act too professional an' he gave dat tomato man a big apologize. Doc Troyhorn say, "I tole him dat I been in de mental health business a long time an' I done seen an' hear it all, but I ain't nava seen nothin' like dat, an' I'm sorry I don't act professional, but dem tomato plant stuck out his ears jus' surprise me.

"De fella look me square in de eye an' say, 'Doc, don't feel bad. I was jus' as surprise as you wan I took a look in de mirrow dis mornin', 'cause I planted pumkins.'"

WIMPY GETS BRAVE

Dere was a fella named Wimpy Savoy dat was one of de easiestgoin' folks 'round Breaux Bridge. In fack, he was so easy he got de nickname "Wimpy" for bein' so easygoin'.

Granpa tole me Doc Troyhorn went into T'Bub's one day an' axed, "Did I hear rite, my patient, Wimpy Savoy, finally took up for hisseff afta he been to see me for a few visit?"

T'Bub say, "Doc, was you de one behin' all dat? Whoo yi yi, nobody could believe deir eyes."

Doc Troyhorn say, "Yeah, I was de one behin' it all. Now don't waste no time, an' gave me all de detail."

T'Bub start to 'splain, "Well, Wimpy was sat rite dere," pointin' to de stool nex to Doc Trayhorn, "an' dis big, ugly, mean-lookin' fella come sit hisseff down rite ware you are sit now, Doc. An', Doc, averybody was mine deir own business wan all a sudden, *kachoom,* dat fella let go on Wimpy, an' po' ole Wimpy hit de floor, den de fella look at Wimpy an' say, 'Dat was a sample of Judo. I learn dat in Japan.'"

T'Bub continue, "Ole Wimpy pick hisseff up an' say, 'Well, boy, dat stuff feel like it work good, I garontee.' Well, Doc, a few drank later dat fella let go again on ole Wimpy wit' one of dem Chinese chop an' Wimpy hit de floor again. Dat fella look at Wimpy an' tole him, 'Dat was a sample of dat Tae Kwon Do. I learn dat in Korea.'"

T'Bub say, "Well, Doc, ole Wimpy pull hisseff back up on de stool an' tole dat fella, 'Dat one feel like it work bedder dan de first one.' Well, Doc, a few more drank was downed, an' low an' behold, dat fella jump up an' put a smashin' blow on ole Wimpy, den he tole Wimpy, 'Dat was a sample of Kung Fu. I learn dat in China.'"

T'Bub say, "Doc, Wimpy don't said a word, he jus' stagger out de door, goin' home. Averytang got all calm down an' was goin' long fine wan all a sudden I heard a *kachoom, kaboom, splat,* an' wan I turn 'round dere stood Wimpy who looked at me an' say, 'T'Bub, wan dat fella woke up, tole him dat was crowbar, an' I got it at Landry's Hardware.'"

CHAPTER 6
Poo Poo an' Stinky

POO POO
ZOOMO OILS
FIREBALL BEARINGS
PINT WHEELS
DAVE'S FENDER
OPD
STINKIES GARAGE
BFD CAMS

RACE DAY

I only put two story 'bout Dr. Troyhorn 'cause I am anxious to tell y'all 'bout de two Arceneaux (prounounced R. C. No) brothers, Poo Poo an' Stinky. I guess one of de bess stories Granpa ava tole me 'bout dem two boys was de time dey 'round up dis flashy '55 Chevy wit' de big 283 V8 c.i.d. motor an' decide to made demseff into professional race-car drivers. Dem work work on dat car day an' night gettin' it all fix up wit' de big cam, manifold, 4-barrel carb, roll bar—averytang. Wan dey got averytang all fine tune dey head out for de race track dat was havin' a 500 mile race wit' a $500 purse for first place, plus dat big gold trophy, whoo yi yi, talk 'bout it made you have to put some sunglass on, it shine so brite. Wan dey got back home averybody in T'Bub's was ax dem, "How you boys did?"

Wit' a look of gloom an' doom, Poo Poo say, "I tole Stinky de nex time he was gonna drive an' I was gonna be de pit stop boy."

Averybody say, "Well, Poo Poo, answer de question, how y'all did?"

Poo Poo say, "I run dead, lass but I woulda won if I didn't have to made dem 75 pit stop."

All at de same time averybody in T'Bub's say, "Seventy-five pit stop! Why de worl' you have to stop dat many times?"

Poo Poo say, "Well, I have to stop 4 time for gas, 4 time for new tire, an' 2 time to got de oil check out."

Averybody say, "Well, dat's jus' 10 stop. How 'bout dem odder 65 stop?"

Poo Poo say, "Well, y'all jus' ain't nava been in fass movin', smokin', noisy traffics like I was drive in. I got confuse quite a few time an' have to stop an' got some directions."

ROCKET FUEL
NO SMOKIN
S
A
USE
UNLEADED
CHECK
OIL

Rocket Fuel

I axed my granpa one time if Doc Troyhorn aver tried to did a study on Poo Poo an' Stinky. Granpa tole me no, but he stayed afta dem all de time, 'cause dey nava held a job or stay in de same place for more dan a couple of months befo dey got fired or kick out for not payin' de rent. De one case dat made Doc water at de mouth to study was wan dey land a job at a rocket factory. De job dey have was pumpin' gas, but at lease dey did get a job wit' rockets. De gossip goin' 'round was Poo Poo an' Stinky was fillin' up dis rocket an' a few drop of gas spill over so, instead of got a rag, Poo Poo wipe de spill wit' his finger an' den lick it. Dat got him all excite an' he axed Stinky, "You know wat we pumpin' here?"

Stinky say, "Yeah, Poo Poo, we pumpin' rocket gas."

Poo Poo say, "No, dat's ware you wrong. We pumpin' pure dee white lighten like daddy make in his still back home." Stinky got him a finger wet, took a lick an' say, "Brother, you are 100 percent rite, dat's all dat is. Go got us two glasses."

Poo Poo an' Stinky sat dere an' each fill dem a glass full of dat rocket gas, drunk it down, an' fanished fillin' up de rocket. Dat night Stinky was jus' tuckin' hisseff in bed wan de phone rang, an' it was Poo Poo, who axed him rite off, "Stinky, do you feel funny or have anytang strange happen wit' you?"

Stinky say, "No, I'm fixin' to go to bed. Why you ax me dat, Poo Poo?"

Poo Poo say, "Well, took my advise an' don't drank anytang dat might made you belch."

Stinky say, "Why you call to tole me dat dis late, Poo Poo?"

Poo Poo say, "'Cause dat's 'zackly wat I done an' I'm callin' you from California."

Race Day Taxes

Dat race day turned out to cost Poo Poo an' Stinky way more dan jus' lass place at de track. It got dem in bad trouble wit' de IRS or, like my granpa call dem, de SRI folks.

It seem wat happen afta dey fix up dat car an' didn't win a dime wit' it, Poo Poo an' Stinky took dem a vacation trip an' claim dat as a medical expense on deir taxes. Well, wit' dem two's luck deir names got pulled out of de "check-dem-out" hat at de SRI office. Wan dey went in for de meetin', de SRI man tole dem, "Dis trip y'all took to New Orleans says it was a medical trip, but I don't see one doctor, hospital, or medicine bill to go wit' dat claim, so all us folk at de SRI office want you to 'splain dat to us."

Well, Poo Poo say, "Mr. SRI man, is like dis, me an' my brother Stinky here got us a fine '55 Chevy wit' de big 283 V8 engine, an' we put all de special race stuff Quality Auto Parts place have to sell on it. We put de special cam, special manifold, de special carburator, averytang we could get to made dat car go as fass as it could. You wit' me so far?"

De SRI fella jus' nod his head. Poo Poo say, "Well, we put all dem part on credit 'cause we figger wan we won de $500 first place prize money an' dat big trophy we could pay dat part bill off, an' still have de car an' trophy."

De SRI man say, "But you still got to 'splain wit' me how dat trip was a medical expense."

Stinky tap Poo Poo on de shoulder an' say, "Brother, let me talk a while." Stinky say, "Well, mista, let me 'splain dat to you. De fella wat own dat Quality Auto Part place is one mean motor-scooter, dat loves to fight, named Emile Breaux. Emile sent out word dat if he saw us in town he was gonna kill us if we didn't pay him for all dem parts."

Man in New York

I guess my favorite Poo Poo Arceneaux story of all is 'bout de time Poo Poo took a trip up to New York City to see if it was all it was crack up to be. Granpa say, "He didn't rememba de name of de hotel he stayed at, but from wat he tole me, it sure wasn't de fanciest one New York had to offer. From wat I gathered, Poo Poo must have drove de fella at de hotel desk crazy in de week he was dere, so de fella wanted to get back to ole Poo Poo befo he leff." Granpa say, "As Poo Poo was checkin' out, de desk fella say, 'My fran, befo you leave I got to ax you dis question. If my mama an' daddy have a baby, an' it wasn't my brother or my sister, who was dat?'"

Well, y'all could jus' 'bout magine how much ole Poo Poo was squirm an' scratch his head, an' he say, "Wooo aaaa," an' afta 'bout 30 minute de desk fella axed, "Mista, you gave up?"

Poo Poo say, "You doggone rite I gave up, I sure ain't too good at dem word kinda question, I garontee."

De hotel fella say, "Dat was me."

Poo Poo taught 'bout dat for 'bout 10 minute an' den he say, "Oh, now I got it, doggone fella, you sure have me goin' dere for a while."

Well, Poo Poo leff de hotel an' got on his plane, an' wan he land in Breaux Bridge, de whole family was dere to met him an' ax him question 'bout dat New York City. De first one to run an' met him was his mama but befo she could grab an' kiss him, Poo Poo push her away an' say, "Mama, please don't did dat rite now 'cause I might plum forgot de question I need to ax you."

Poo Poo's mama say, "Well, ax me, cher."

Poo Poo say, "O.K., if you an' daddy have a baby an' it wasn't my brother or my sister, who was dat?"

Well, dere goes his mama squirm an' scratch her head, sayin' "Wooo aaaa." She even axed his daddy an' his brother, Stinky, an' have dem all squirm an' scratch. Afta 'bout 20 minute de mama say, "Poo Poo, we don't know, we jus' can't figure out de answer to dat question. Who was dat?"

Poo Poo puff his chess out an' say, "Dat was a fella who work at a hotel desk in New York City."

CHAPTER 7
Holidays

32
BBHS

FOOTBALL

I will admit my favorite day of de year is Superbowl Sunday 'cause, numba one, I love football, an', numba two, Boo Boo (dat's my wife) is gonna fix up my favorite meal, red beans an' rice.

It seems dat de people on de T.V. dat film de games always want to play an' show de real hard hits an' tackles over an' over again. I will admit dat averytime dey play one of dem hard hits it brings to mine a story my granpa tole me 'bout li'l Wimpy Savoy. Granpa say dey called de daddy Wimpy 'cause he wasn't de John Wayne type for sure, an' his boy, li'l Wimpy, was jus' like 'em but he played football anyhow.

Well, de story goes dat li'l Wimpy was on de third or fourth string at Breaux Bridge High School's football team an' dey was playin' dis team from 'round Lake Charles dat have a boy who could chew barbed wire like bubble gum, he was so tough an' mean. Well, dat boy done knock out de first string boy, de second string boy, an' li'l Wimpy was on his knees by now prayin', "Lord, please don't let de coach call out my name. Dat boy's gonna hurt me bad." Well, dat prayer got cut short 'cause de Breaux Bridge coach yell, "Li'l Wimpy Savoy, got in dere, we need you."

Li'l Wimpy walk out on de field an' Granpa say on de first play dat boy hit Wimpy, *kachoom,* wit' a forearm an' off de field come li'l Wimpy screamin', "Coach, he knocked me blind. Please took me out, I can't see nothin' but a blur, it's like I'm lookin' true a funnel."

De coach yell back, "Li'l Wimpy, you O.K. Don't be scare 'cause you ain't blind, you jus' lookin' true de earhole on you helmet."

ROBICHAW
Robichaw
RIP
Robichaw

Mr. Romance

Accordin' to my wife Boo Boo, de biggest day in any women's life is wan dey are axed de question to marry by de man dey love. Well, dis story always leaves my Boo Boo in stitches wan I tell folks wat my granpa tole me 'bout ole Boom Robichaw (pronounced Robe A Shaw).

It seem like Boom (dey call him dat 'cause he always have a firecracker stan' set up for de fourth of July, New Year, etc.) start goin' out wit' MeMe Babineaux, one of de twin ole maids in Breaux Bridge dat was always man-huntin' wit' her sister Ava. One night, 'bout 1 A.M., MeMe come knockin' down Ava's bedroom door to tole her de big news. MeMe say, "Sis, woke up, I got sometang to show you an' sometang to tole you at de same time."

Ava flip on de light an' sat up in de bed to put on her glasses an' see wat her sister MeMe was so excite 'bout. MeMe push dat ⅛ carrot rang in Ava's face an' say, "Sis, Boom ax me to marry him, an' look at dat rang he gave me."

Well, Ava jump out de bed wit' all kinda excitement for her sister, MeMe. Afta de excitement calm down, Ava say, "Sis, tell me all 'bout wat happen. Did Boom brung you out to a beautiful spot on de bayou, wit' de moon shinin' true de moss on de cypress trees, take you hand, tell you he loved you an' dat he couldn't live witout you?"

MeMe say, "No, dat ain't wat happen."

Ava say, "Well, don't kep me waitin', wat happen?"

MeMe say, "Well, tonite Boom tole me he didn't have no money to go out, so we went over his house an' he have all de fixin' for me to made a pot of red bean an' rice. Well, while I was in de kitchen up to my neck in cookin' dem beans, Boom was layin' on de sofa watchin' de rasslin' on T.V. An' wan de commercial come on he call me in de room an' ax me to be his bride."

Ava say, "Sis, jus' wat were de words he used?"

MeMe say, "Well, he jus' come rite out an' say 'MeMe, cher, how would you like to be buried in my family's cemetary plot?"

Gobble Turkey

Dis is not a Cajun story, but I taught it was jus' too cute to not share wit' my readers.

Dere was dis li'l turkey named Gobble, an' boy, he got into averytang out in de barnyard. Well, one day Gobble was beside hisseff, he was run all 'round de barnyard gettin' into trouble, an' knockin' over all de odder animals' food an' water dishes. De more his mama fussed, de more he got into. Wan his mama was finally at her wit's end she stood firm, wit' her wings on her thighs, an' she shouted, "Gobble, if you daddy could see how you actin' up now, he would roll over in his gravy."

HAPPY
VALEN
TINE

Valentine No No

My granpa always gave me good sound advise, like nava go back on you word, pay people wat you owe dem on time, be good to you family, wan you shook hands on somethin' de deal is done, an' nava buy you wife or girlfriend laundry for Valentine's Day.

De lass one I didn't quite undastood an' I axed him, "Granpa, wat you mean by laundry?"

He tole me, "Dem sexy nightgown an' clothes like dat."

I say, "Oh, you mean lingerie. Why shouldn't I buy dat, Granpa?"

Granpa tole me one year wan dey was young, he got my granma some of dem laundry nightgown an' she didn't spoke to him for 'bout tree week. I axed him why he taught she got so mad.

Granpa say, "Well, cher, dat's been a long, long time ago, an' to dis day I still don't know if it was de red flannel or drop-down back she didn't like de most."

Expensive Bird

Granpa always tole dis story wan de bird was served on one of de holidays.

Dere was a fella named Pup Landry (Pup was a nickname dat came 'bout 'cause he was dog breeder an' always had some puppies for sale) dat got rich overnight wan oil was found on his land. Granpa say dat ole Pup was a real nice fella, but dat oil money change him like night an' day. Afta dat oil was found he always wanted to be de big shot an' brag 'bout how much money he have.

To got back to de story Granpa always tole, it came from de first Tanksgivin' dat Pup have money an' went to see ole Badeaux (pronounced Bay Doe) at de pet store. Pup went in an' axed ole Badeaux, "Wat's de most expensive bird you got in here?"

Badeaux say, "Oh, Pup, let me show you wat I got."

Badeaux showed Pup dis parrot dat was 'bout four foot long, head to tail, an' he 'splain dat bird was one of de rarest bird in de whole worl', 'cause dey didn't have but 100 of dem leff. He showed Pup all de colors he have, 'bout 20 in all, an' den Badeaux start talkin' wit' dat bird. Dat bird could carry on a conversatin' jus' like he was a people. Den Badeaux tole Pup, "'Cause of all dat, he cost you for $10,000."

Pup say, "Now, Badeaux, you promise me dat's de mos expensive bird dey got, huh?"

Badeaux say, "You won't fine no bird anyware dat coss more dan dis one, I garontee."

Pup say, "O.K., I'll took him, but you need to answer de most important question."

Badeaux say, "If I can. Wat question is dat?"

Pup say, "Dat question is dis. Is he tender?"

CHAPTER 8
Kepin' de Faith

18
JACKO
LEON

De Golf Game

Father DeBlue was always numba one in de Catholic community, but for dose folks in Breaux Bridge, dat weren't nobody was betta den Brother Begno Bourgeois (pronounced Booge Wah). Father DeBlue an' Brother Begno were real good frans, both bein' men of de cloth, an' always respected each odder quite a bit. Father DeBlue an' Brother Begno were also both big golf fans an' played together often. One day, out on de golf course, dey decide it might be a good idea to have a big golf tournament between deir two congregations to brung fellowship to Breaux Bridge.

Well, won't you know, de Pope over in Rome got a wiff of wat was goin' on, an' he call Father DeBlue personally an' tole him he was gonna sand over a nice Catholic fella named Leon Travineaux to help him out. De Pope also tole DeBlue to call him afta dey fanish de numba 18 hole an' gave him de result. DeBlue say, "You Holiness, you could count on me, as soon as de 18 hole is played, I'll be on de phone wit' you, I garontee."

Well, de big day finally arrived, an' de golf game started, an' jus' as he promise, Father DeBlue was on de phone to Rome to gave de Pope de update on de game. DeBlue say, "You Holiness, dey jus' fanish dat numba 18 hole an' de score is dead tie. We gonna have to play a numba 19, or maybe more, to fine out who won."

De Pope axed Father DeBlue, "How is dat Leon Travineaux fella I sent you doin'?"

Father DeBlue say, "Oh, he's did fine, an' I garontee he's one of de bess golfer I aver seen in my life, but ole Brother Begno Bourgeois has a fella on his team name Jacko Nicaulas dat ain't too bad either."

De Angel Lit de Candle

Most of de folks in Breaux Bridge today are Catholic, jus' as all deir forefathers befo dem. Granpa always tole me one of de most respected men in Breaux Bridge wan he was growin' up was de priest, Father DeBlue. Granpa always tole me stories 'bout Father DeBlue an' dis one is rite dere in de top 10.

It seems dat li'l Cush Cush Quibodeaux (pronounced Kwib Oh Do) had jus' fanish his alter boy trainin' an' was jus' 'bout to serve his first mass an', whoo yi yi, he was a nervous wreck. Father DeBlue had been a priest for a long time an' he knew jus' wat poor Cush Cush was goin' true. Granpa say, to calm him down, Father DeBlue took li'l Cush Cush, sat him down, an' ax him why he was so nervous. Li'l Cush Cush say, "Father, I know de whole mass, but I always got confuse an' forgot to lite dat big candle wan I'm suppose to."

Father DeBlue laugh an' say, "Is dat why you so nervous, cher? Well, don't you be worry 'bout dat, I done train a whole bunch of li'l fellas like you an' we gonna did fine."

Father DeBlue say, "O.K., li'l Cush Cush, wan you hear me sang 'An' de Angel Lit de Candle,' dat's de time you go lite dat candle."

Li'l Cush Cush say, "O.K., Father, I'm gonna be listen for dat an' real good, too."

De mass was goin' fine an' de time come for Cush Cush to lite dat candle. Father DeBlue sang, "An' de Angel Lit de Candle." Dare was no Cush Cush so he repeat, "An' de Angel Lit de Candle." Still no Cush Cush. Now Father was half mad an' half worry, so he sang real loud, "*An' de Angel Lit de Candle.*" All a sudden a voice from behin' him sang, "De Angle wanted to lite de candle, but de alter boy spilt de water an' wine all over de matches."

Hospital Visits

Doctors all have to made deir way 'round de hospital to took care of deir patients' medical needs, but Granpa say averyone could always depand on Father DeBlue or Brother Begno to drop in to say hello an' took care of deir spiritual needs.

Granpa tole me dat Father DeBlue was made his visit to de hospital an' he go by ole Sparky Prevost's room, was jus' have his appendix, or as Granpa called it, pendix, took out. Sparky was lay dere an' wan ole Father DeBlue come in de room, much to his suprise, Sparky was his happy-go-lucky seff.

Sparky say, "Hey dere, Father. I'm glad you come by to pass a visit wit' me."

Father DeBlue say, "Well, Sparky, I'm glad to see you doin' so good afta dat surgery, an' you even got dat Sparky smile an' attitude afta all you been true."

Sparky say, "Well, ain't no reason to be sad an' unhappy, 'cause ole Doc Duplichan took care of me, an' I ain't in no pain now like I was wan dey brung me here."

Sparky den axed Father DeBlue if he wouldn't mine did him a favor.

Father DeBlue say, "I'll be glad to help you if I could. Wat you need?"

Sparky look up at dat drip bag an' tube dat Doc Duplichan had dem put in his arm an' say, "Well, Father DeBlue, I knew you an' ole Doc Duplichan is good frans, an' dere ain't much you could ax him for he wouldn't did for you, ain't dat rite?"

Father DeBlue say, "Sparky, I guess dat depand on wat I ax. Wat you got in mine?"

Sparky say, "Ax him to gave me a extra bag an' tube like I got in my arm. I seen a nice lookin' lady in de room 'cross de hall an' I was tinkin' 'bout axin' her over for lunch."

4x4 Truck

In times of a serious medical crisis, us Catholics always want a priest by our bedside givin' us de lass rites. Dem rites gave us a chance to pass away wit' a clean slate. Well, ole Father DeBlue, on his hospital visits, was always dere to pray for an' administer de lass rites to people in need.

Well, one day ole Father DeBlue was made his hospital rounds an' he go in to pass a visit on ole Val Babin, one of de most avid hunters in Breaux Bridge, dat had come down wit' a bad case of knee-monia out in de cold, frozen marsh while duck huntin' in weather dat would sand cold shivers down a polar bear's back. While ole Father DeBlue was talkin' wit' Val, he axed him if he needed him for anytang special.

Val say, "Yeah, Father, I'd like for you to gave me de lass rites jus' in case dat knee-monia get real bad an' took me out."

Father DeBlue say, "Well, Val, dat's a good idea, averybody oughta taught like dat, 'cause dere ain't no garontee you gonna be here to see de nex sunrise."

Father DeBlue fanish gave Val de lass rites an' den he axed him if he need anytang else.

Val say, "Yeah, Father, dere is one more tang dat's been on my mine."

Father DeBlue say, "Wat's dat, Val?"

Val say, "Well, Father, averybody in my family gots a whole lotta respeck for you an' dey gonna listen to wat you tell dem, so please tell dem I wanna be bury in my 4x4 truck if anytang happen. Could you did dat for me?"

Father DeBlue say, "Yeah, Val, I could tell dem dat for you, but I gotta ax you, why de worl' would you request sometang like dat?"

Val say, "Well, Father, you know me an' my partner, Goose, love to hunt an' we done gone to places ain't nobody been to hunt."

Father DeBlue say, "Yeah, I know dat, but dat still don't answer de question, why you wanna be bury in you 4x4 truck?"

Val say, "'Cause I ain't nava seen a hole my 4x4 truck couldn't pull me out of."

CHAPTER 9
De Hunters

I'M GOIN' HUNTIN'

Granpa always talked 'bout dese two fellas named Val Babin an' Goose Bourgeois (pronounced Booge Wah) bein' de two most avid hunters in de Breaux Bridge area. In fack, Granpa tole me both of dem had been fire from jobs 'cause dey jus' couldn't fine it in deir hearts to be workin' on a job durin' de huntin' season.

Well, one huntin' season Val's wife, Frances, done filled up to her eyeballs listenin' to de huntin' stories dem two nava stop talkin' 'bout, an' she made up her mine tangs was gonna be a li'l bit different dis huntin' season. On openin' day, Val was up at 3 A.M., an' low an' behold, he walk into de kitchen to put on de coffee an' dere sat Frances, already sippin' on her a cup, all dress up in huntin' clothes she had dug up for herseff outa Val's huntin' clothes closet.

Val took one look an' axed Frances, "Ware you taught you goin'?"

Frances say, "I'm goin' huntin', Val."

Val say, "Is dat rite?"

Frances say, "You doggone rite I'm goin' huntin' wit' you, 'cause I'm tired of bein' a huntin' widow avery year wit' you stuck out dere in de woods an' me here all by myseff."

Val say, "Well, Frances, got dat notion out you head, 'cause you ain't goin' huntin' wit' me an' Goose."

Granpa tole me Frances was one of dem easy goin', life lovin', sweet kinda people, but you would have a betta chance fightin' a chainsaw den to tangle wit' Frances wan she got her temper up.

Frances got rite up in Val's face an' tole him, "If I can't hunt, you for sure ain't goin'."

Well, Val knew from lookin' in her face it was not de time to gave Frances any back sass, so all he could did was say, "O.K., let's go."

So dey got in de 4x4 truck, passed by Goose's house to pick him up, an' head out to de woods. De whole time dey was drive, Goose kep flash dem eyes at Val as if to say, "Wat de worl' is Frances doin' here?" Val gave dat look back as if to say, "Dis is gonna be de lass time she goes, 'cause we gonna fix her up an' real good."

Dey finally got out to deir favorite deer huntin' spot an' Val proceeded to get Frances all fix up in de highest tree he could fine dat don't have no branches to block out dat cold nort wind dat was blowin', an' he fix her deer stan' seat an' tole her, "Now you gotta sit here an' be real, real quiet, an' don't move or dat deer ain't gonna come no ware in sight. Now you got dat?"

Frances say, "Yeah, I got dat. Beside, afta listen to you an' Goose talk all dem year, I know 'zackly wat's goin' on."

Val say, "O.K., Frances, you on you own," an' he leff to go set up his stan'.

Val hadn't walk 200 yard wan he hear *Boom! Boom!* comin' from back ware he leff Frances, so he turn 'round an' start high tail it back, an' de closer he got he start heard Frances' voice sayin', "I shot him, he's mine, an' you can't have 'em." De closer he got, de more clear he could heard Frances, an' again' he heard her voice, but dis time loud an' clear, "*He's mine, I shot him, an' you can't have 'em!*"

Den Val heard a man's voice dat say, "'Mam, I'm not gonna argue wit' you while you got dat gun point at me, but all I'm axin' is for you to let me took my saddle off him."

Off-Season Jobs

I done wrote 'bout ole Val, but ain't mentioned Goose 'sept he was Val's huntin' partner. Goose nava got marry, an' he didn't have to answer to a wife like Val have to answer to Frances, so he pretty much could do wat he want, like stayin' on a job till huntin' season roll 'round, den quit to be out in de woods. In one of de off-season, Goose got hisseff a job at Henry LeJuene's gas station doin' oil change an' odder odd job like dat. It was dat odd job dat got dis story goin' 'round Breaux Bridge, an' I'm not only glad my granpa heard it, I'm also glad he tole me 'bout it so I can pass it on to you.

It seems like dis yankee couple was passin' true Breaux Bridge an' saw de town name sign. De couple, bein' yankees, didn't 'zackly know how to pronounce dat name, so dey pull over into Henry's ware ole Goose was sweepin' up de parkin' lot an' axed him, "Mista, we ain't from 'round here an' we wanna know jus' how to prounounce de name of dis place. Is it Bree X or Bree O?"

Goose say, "It ain't neither one of dem. You pronounce dis place [sayin' it slow] F-I-L-L-I-N' S-T-A-T-I-O-N."

NKY'S

Don't Hunt Elephants or Whale

Granpa tole me 'bout de time dis big-shot reporter fella came to Breaux Bridge to did a report 'bout de huntin' in Louisiana, an' afta talkin' wit' a bunch of folk he found out 'bout Val an' Goose bein' de two most avid hunters in de state. So he search dem out an' wound up in T'Bub's drinkin' a few suds an' talkin' wit' Val an' Goose.

Afta hearin' 'bout 100 huntin' stories, dat reporter fella say, "Well, you boys are 'zackly wat I been lookin' for, I garontee, but I got to ax y'all dis question. Is dere anytang y'all don't hunt?"

Val an' Goose look at each odder an' say, "No, we hunt jus' 'bout anytang, deer, squirrel, duck, nutra, coon, turkey, boar." Den Val say, "Wait jus' a minute, dere is two tangs we won't hunt, an' dat's whales or elephant. We don't, an' won't, hunt dem."

Dat reporter fella say, "An' why is dat? Y'all wanna save de whale, an' not kill de elephant to steal de ivory from his tusk?"

Goose say, "Mah no, it ain't 'cause of dat!"

De reporter fella say, "Well den, why?"

Val an' Goose together say, "My fran, if you aver tried to pull either one of dem tangs into a piroque [prouounced pee-row, a cajun canoe], you would know 'zackly why we won't hunt either one of dem tangs again."

CHAPTER 10
Philosea

At de Track

De first grade elementary school teacher in Breaux Bridge, Louisiana, was named Philosea (pronounced Phil O She Ah) Thibodaux (pronounced Tib Ah Do) an' one day she decide to took all dem li'l first grade folks to de Evangeline Downs horse racetrack to taught dem all 'bout dem horse. Afta a while, all dem li'l first grade folk have to go use de potty, so Miss Thibodaux axed dis fella stood 'round, "Is dere a batroom 'round here dat de publics don't use dat I could brung all dem li'l boys to?"

De fella say, "Oh yes, mam, go down dat hall rite dere an' use dat batroom. De publics don't use dat one at all."

Miss Thibodaux march all dem li'l fella down de hall an' she was goin' down de line help all dem li'l fella tuck in deir shirt, zip up deir zipper, an' buckle up deir belts. Averytang was goin' fine till she got to dis one li'l fella an' she took a step back an' say, "Whoo yi yi, cher, are you in de first?"

Dat li'l fella turn 'round an' in a deep voice proclaimed, "No, mam, I'm ridin' Cajun Queen in de fifth."

January 12,
TUESDAY
H_2O = Water
H =
O =
Elmo ✓✓✓
margeaux ✓✓✓
Poupou ✓✓✓✓✓
Fideaux ✓
LV
BR
LESSON
PLAN

Science Spearmint

One day Miss Philosea Thibodaux tole her first grade class dey was gonna did a science spearmint. Miss Thibodaux reach in a li'l cigar box full of dirt an' pull out dis earthworm, an' say, "O.K., y'all watch wat happen wan I put dis worm in 100 percent pure dee water." She drop dat li'l worm in dat glass an, whoo, he was have some fun swimmin' all 'round in dat glass, I garontee.

Afta a few minute, Miss Thibodaux took dat worm out de water an' she say, "O.K., y'all watch wat happen wan I put dis li'l worm in 100 percent pure dee alcohol." Miss Thibodaux put dat worm in dat alcohol an' he swim 'round, but afta a few minute dat worm stop swimmin' an' stiff up like a 4x2 board an' passed away in de glass.

Miss Thibodaux say, "O.K., class, now wat dat spearmint prove?"

De first one to push his hand in de air was li'l Skinny Chenet (pronounced Shin-A). Miss Thibodaux say, "O.K., Skinny, wat dat prove?"

Li'l Skinny say, "Miss Thibodaux, dat prove if you drank 'nuff of dat alcohol you nava gonna have de worms, I garontee!"

CHAPTER 11
Lagniappe (A Li'l Extra)

Jealous Brothers

Dey have dese two twin brothers named Don O. Ville an' Dan O. Ville wat was always tryin' to out did each odder. One year Don O. Ville fine out dat Dan O. Ville bought deir mama a bran' new Cataract car for her birthday an', whoo, he didn't like dat none at all, so he go out to dis pet store an' bought dis Mina Bird dat could spoke 13 language, includin' Franch, an' sent it to his mama special delivery on de USP truck.

Don O. Ville call his mama de nex day an' axed her how she liked dat bird. His Mama say, "Whoo, cher, dat bird made de bess gumbo we aver made here at de house!"

Don O. Ville got all axcite an' say, "Mama, dat bird could talk 13 language, he coss me $10,000, an' you made gumbo outa him?!"

His mama say, "Well, cher, if he was dat smart, why he didn't said sometang?!"

Do It Youseffer

I'll nava forgot de time Granpa tole me 'bout wan he went to visit his fran Sosta Melançon in de hospital an' rite across de hall he spot his ole fran Beans Bergeron, who was in dat traction, Granpa say. His neck was in a brace, his arms was in casts, an' he have black-n-blue spots all over him from head to toe. Granpa say he went in an' axed Beans if he got de tag number of de tank wat rolled over him?

Beans say, "Ain't dat a fine mess I'm in, Gilbear?"

Granpa say, "Beans, how in de worl' did all dis happen?"

Beans say, "It was a carpenter accident."

Granpa say, "Carpenter accident!? Beans, you gotta tole me 'bout dis."

Beans tole Granpa dat him an' his wife been taught 'bout buildin' demseff a new house for a long time, an' wan dey have all de money save up dey go down to de lumber yard an' buy dis three story house kit, 'cause he figure wit' him did all de labor dey could ford to build a three story house instead of two.

Granpa say, "Beans, you ain't no carpenter!"

He say, "Yeah, I know dat now, Gilbear." Den he continue to tole Granpa how he lay out all dem blue prints (but since de accident Beans call dem black-n-blue prints), an' he start goin' to town on dat house.

Granpa say, "Well, Beans, tell me 'bout de accident."

Beans say, "Well, Gilbear, I still don't know ware I went wrong, but yesterday I walked in de front door an' fell off de roof."

Papa's Advise

Almost averybody who is Cajun knows wat Cajun daddies always tole deir boys befo dey get married, but for you non-Cajun readers, I'm gonna tole y'all 'bout de time ole man Begno Benoit (pronounced Ben Wah) sit his oldest son, Begno Jr., down an' tole him, "Boy, it's 'bout time for you to start lookin' for a wife an' give me some granchildrens to play wit'. But befo you start lookin', I want to tole you three important tangs you gotta tink 'bout:

Numba one, made sure dat girl could cook good, 'cause dat's wat you gonna be eatin' for de ress of you life.

Numba two, made for sure dat girl loves an' wants planty babies for me an' you mama to play wit' an' spoil rotten.

Numba three, dis is de mos important tang—Son, took a long hard look at dat girl's mama, 'cause dat's wat she's gonna look like in 30 years!"

Mama's Advise

I will admit, however, dat very few folks, not even Cajun men, know wat de Cajun girl's advise from deir mama is, but afta a whole bunch of private eye, undacover, an' smart maneuverin'—more commonly called beggin'—I found out for you. Wan a Cajun girl is fixin' to get married her mama will brung her off to de side an' tole her, "Wan you husband comes home afta work sit him down in a tick-tick-tick cushion easy chair, prop his feet high on a footstool, an' brung him sometang cold to drank."

De girls always say, "But, Mama, if I did dat, it's gonna spoil dat man rotten."

Den de mama's advise come into de picture an' changes dem girl's minds averytime. De mamas always tell dem girls dey nava gonna believe how much money is gonna fall out deir husband's pants in between de cushions in dat chair wan dey did dat.

LOUSIANA STATE CENTER

Hospitality Champion

I take a lot of pride in being Cajun, an' I'm equally as proud to be Southern. Wan you put Cajun an' Southern together you can only come up wit' someone who loves life, food, family, God, an' showin' people friendship an' hospitality—but *no one* can top Alex Prejean, who owns an' operates a restaurant in Lafayette, Louisiana. Alex acquired his Hospitality Champion title one day wan a bus driver came into his restaurant an' tole Alex he was from de mental hospital an' had some of de patients out for a sightseein' tour for de day. De driver also 'splained averyone was hungry an' wanted to come in to eat. De driver also 'splained de folks in de bus would try to pay deir bills wit' bottlecaps an' axed Alex to please not laugh at dem but take deir bottlecaps an' wan averyone was back on de bus he would come in to pay de bill.

Alex say, "Please brung in all dem folks. We will be more dan happy to feed dem."

The driver emptied de bus an' Alex emptied de kitchen, bringin' dose folks gumbo, dirty rice, boiled shrimp, boiled crawfish, complete wit' corn an' potatoes, etc., etc., etc., an' topped dem all off wit' beignets an' coffee. De driver was correct, an' averyone started pullin' deir bottlecaps out for Alex, who was smilin' an' thankin' dem all for deir business. De driver rounded up averyone, got dem back on de bus, an' came back in to pay Alex, but not befo tankin' dem for all de wonderful food, service, an' hospitality. Alex proudly exclaimed, "Anytime, my fran. We will be happy to have dem folks in anytime!"

De driver den looked Alex in de eyes an' say, "Well, it's time to pay you. I sure hope you have change for a hubcap."

FILE

Shipwrecked Cajun

One day ole Achille Landry was out in his shrimpboat wan a big ole squall came up dat true him an' de boat up on dis li'l island nobody knew 'bout. Low an' behold, dis lady who was out cruisin' in her boat got caught in de same squall an' wash up on dat same island wit' nothin' but a li'l black bag. Achille had to nurse dat lady back to health, 'cause dat squall had beat her up pretty bad.

Afta she was back on her feet, dat lady one day axed Achille, "Befo you got shipwreck, did you drank?"

Achille say, "Oh yes, mam, I drank." So she reach in dat li'l black bag an' pull out a bottle of wine.

Den she axed Achille, "Befo you got shipwreck, did you like filé gumbo?"

Achille say, "Oh yes, mam, I love filé gumbo." So she reach in dat li'l black bag an' pull out a fresh jar of filé.

Den dat lady bat her eyelash an' axed Achille, in a sexy tone of voice, "Befo you got shipwreck, did you play 'round?"

Achille got de biggest smile wat you aver saw on his face an' say, "Mam, don't tole me you got a set of golf club in dat bag, too!"

De Lass Straw

One evenin', afta a long, hot day of brick layin, ole Flash LeBlanc come draggin' in de house only to see Uncle J. D. kick back in his easy chair watchin' de T.V.

Flash go in de kitchen an' open de ice box an' dat beer he been taught 'bout all day was missin'.

Flash walk back into de livin' room only to see Uncle J. D. drainin' de lass swollow down de bottleneck into his throat. Whoo yi yi, believe you me, you could have fry an' egg on Flash's head, he was so hot!

Flash go down de hall into his bedroom ware his wife, Verna, was sewin' some clothes an' he slam de door an' say, "Verna! I been put up wit' dat man for goin' on seven year but I'm sorry, I don't want him in de house one more day, so march down dat hall an' brokes de news to him rite now!"

Verna say, "Hole averytang rite dere, Flash. Why I gotta be de one to kick dat poor ole soul out? You de one dat's mad an' want him gone, not me."

Flash say, "Well, I jus' taught it would be betta comin' from you 'cause, afta all, he is you uncle."

Verna say, "Hole on dere, Flash, who say he was my uncle? For de lass seven year I taught he was *you* Uncle!?"

CREDIT CARE

One day Po Boy Fontenot (pronounced Font In No) was showin' René Broussard de new fancy gold credit card he jus' got in de mail. René say, "Oh yeah, I got one of dem tangs befo, but won't you know I loss it!"

Po Boy say, "René, I'm glad you tole me dat, 'cause I been worry 'bout how much red tape I'm gonna half to go true if I loss dat card."

René say, "Well, Po Boy, I can't answer you dat, 'cause I ain't nava report dat tang bein' loss."

Po Boy say, "You ain't nava report dat card bein' loss?! Are you crazy?"

René say, "Not one li'l bit , Po Boy, 'cause whoaver found dat card only charge 'bout half wat my wife aver put on it, I garontee!"

SOAP
FLASH
FLASH
FLASH
FLASH
FLASH
FLASH
FLASH
FLASH
FLASH

SOAP COUPONS

Ole T'Boy Arceneaux was brag to his fran, Knute Guidry, all 'bout de bran new $100,000, 10 room house he jus' fanish build for his wife, New Noon. Knute say, "Well, T'Boy, dat's nice, but how much money you taught it's gonna coss you to put furniture in all dem room?"

T'Boy say, "Not one dime for de livin' room an' one for de bedroom."

Knute say, "Wat you mean, not one dime? Did somebody gave y'all dat furniture?"

T'Boy say, "No, Knute, my wife, New Noon, done save up 'nuff of dem coupon she got off some soap box to get dat furniture free."

Knute say, "Well, T'Boy, dat was a good deal, but how 'bout dem odder eight room, wat you 'magine dat's gonna coss you to furnish?"

T'Boy say, "Well, I guess it's gonna be a while befo I find dat out."

Knute say, "Why?"

T'Boy say, "Well, ain't no tellin' how long it's gonna took us to use all de soap in de boxes we got piled up in dem room rite now."

BARRAS
BARBER
SHOP

St. Patrick's Day

De rumor goin' round 'bout us Cajun folks not needin' much of an' excuse to throw a party an' pass a good time is 100 percent trueff, I garontee. Wan St. Patrick's Day comes 'round, we are always more dan happy to join our Irish frans in de celebration, green beer, an' all de trimmin' dat go long wit' it, too.

De one St. Patrick's Day I know Bubby Barras de barber will always remember is 1967, 'cause dat's de one dis fella all dress up in green, wit' shamrock stuck all over his clothes, come into his barber shop wit' his li'l boy an' tole Bubby to gave him de whole makeover, shave, haircut, shampoo, an' shoeshine, 'cause he was celebratin' St. Patrick's Day.

Bubby got fanish wit' de makeover an' de fella tole his li'l boy, "Sean Patrick, come sit in de chair an' let Mr. Barras gave you a haircut while I go down de street an' took care of a li'l business. Den I'll be back to pick you up an' pay Mr. Barras."

Li'l Sean Patrick climb up in de chair an' Bubby gave him de haircut, an' afta he got fanish he tole li'l Sean Patrick to go sit on de bench an' wait for his daddy.

Afta 'bout two hour pass an' de li'l boy was still sat dere, Bubby say, "Well, Sean Patrick, it look like you daddy done got to celebratin' an' plum forgot you, huh?"

De li'l boy say, "Well, I guess I ought to tell you my name ain't Sean Patrick, an' dat fella ain't my daddy!"

Bubby say, "Well, who dat was if he ain't you daddy?"

De li'l fella say, "I don't know, he jus' pass me on de street an' say, 'Boy, if you don't say a word we gonna both got us a free haircut.'"

BBFD
4
BREAX
FIRE DE
DGE

Breaux Bridge Fire Department

My granpa tole me dis story at lease 100 times, like granpas do, but out of respect for him I would have nava stop him an' tole him I heard dat one befo, plus I loved de story den an' tell it averytime I perform now, an' have made tousands of people laugh de way I did wan I was a kid.

Granpa always start off by tellin' me de pride an' joy of Breaux Bridge, Louisiana, is de fire department, an' dat came to be de day wan one of dem oil shiek from Salty Rabie's oil wells caught on fire an' he call avery big shot fire department in de worl' to come put out de fire, but averybody was busy. Den somebody tole de shiek to call de Breaux Bridge fire department, dat dey could put out de oil well fire like dat (a snap of de fingers). So de shiek call an' talk wit' Fire Chief Pa2 Premeaux (prounounced Pre Moe) at de Breaux Bridge fire department.

Pa2 say, "Yeah, we could put out dem oil well fire like dat. Ware you say you at—Ariabi—over dere on de east bank of New Orleans?"

Dat shiek say, "Maah, no, I tole you I'm in Salty Rabie. Dat's way over here in de Middle of de East, half way round de worl' from you dere!"

Pa2 say, "How de worl' we suppose to got way over dere?"

Dat shiek tole Pa2, "Don't worry 'bout dat, we gonna sand a big transport plane to got y'all."

Pa2 say, "Well, how much y'all gonna pay us to put out dat fire?"

Dat shiek tole Pa2, "I'll give y'all for $5 million dolla."

Whoo! Wan he say dat, Pa2 come to attention on de phone an' say, "Mr. Shiek, you sand dat plane, we gonna be ready, I garontee you dat!"

De shiek sand dat transport plane to Breaux Bridge an' wan de put de tailgate down Pa2 loaded de whole fire department on dere, he even brung de dog wat hung 'round de station, ole Blue. Dat plane took off an' land over dere in Salty Rabie, an' dey put dat tailgate down, an' here come de Breaux Bridge fire department. Ole Pa2 got de siren goin' an' de bell a rangin', all de men up top were yellin' an' screamin', an' ole Blue was barkin' his lung out. Pa2 got out to dat fire an' he don't slow down one li'l bit, he drive slap dab into de middle of dat fire an' all de men jump off an' start beat dat fire wit' de rags, an' ole Pa2 was hole dat hose. Why, dey even got ole Blue pushin' de sand between his legs on dat fire. Dey fight dat fire 'bout six hour an' it finally go out.

Well, dat shiek come run over to Fire Chief Pa2 Premeaux wit' big tears of joy in his eyes an' tole him, "Chief, dat's got to be de finest oil well fire fighten' job I aver seen in my life. De way y'all jus' drove in an' took dat fire on an' nava let up till dat fire was out!" Den de shiek hand Pa2 a suitcase wit' dat $5 million dolla inside.

De shiek say, "Chief, I gots to ax you jus' one question. Wat's a li'l town an' li'l fire department like Breaux Bridge gonna did wit' all dat money?"

Fire Chief Pa2 say, "Mr. Shiek, I been taught de same tang an' I taught: de first tang we gonna did is have dem brakes fixed on dat truck!"

No More Worries

If I were given a choice between 40 lashes wit' a whip or goin' to a wake it would be a hard decide to make, I garontee. It is always an awkward time to fine de rite words to say to someone who has jus' loss a beloved family member, unless you're like Sadie Lançon (pronounced Lawn Son), who nava gets at a loss for words. Even if dey are de most tacky an' cold fack words, it jus' don't bother Sadie.

De one dat comes to mine is wan ole Gashouse Gauthreaux (pronounced Go Throw) passed away (dey called him Gashouse 'cause nobody aver wanted to lite a match in de area he was breathin' his 90 proof breath, I garontee!) an' his poor wife, Adrian, was ballin' her eyes out wan here come Sadie Lançon to pay her respeks.

Sadie walk up to poor ole Adrian, gave her a kiss on de cheek, an' say, "Cher, I know you heart is smash to pieces rite now, but it's times like dis you gotta force youseff to look on de brite side."

Adrian say, "Wat brite side, Sadie?"

Sadie say, "Well, at lease now you won't have to worry ware he is at night no more."

ABC
GYM

STOP DE MUSIC

Dis is one of de earliest stories I aver remember my granpa tellin' me, an' I guess y'all will realize how dated dis story is wan you read "ridin' horses to a *fais do do,*" but I still hold it close to my heart as one of my all-time sentimental favorites.

De *fais do do* was goin' strong, wan all a sudden here come ole Felix Hebert (pronounced A Bear) runnin' in an did wat you don't did at a Cajun *fais do do*—he stop de music. Felix jump up on de bandstand an' yell out, "I went to go home an' somebody done paint my horse green, an' I wanna know who dat was, an' I want him up here, an' rite now, too!"

Well, here come dis fella who was 6'5" tall, dat weigh 'bout 275 lb, an' so many scars on his face it look like a road map. He got up in ole Felix face an' say, "I did dat! *Why?*"

Felix eye up dat fella an' say, "I jus' want to tole you she's dry now, an' ready for de second coat."

De Lucky One

Rodney Dangerfield has made de line "I don't get no respect" famous an' I always tink dat line also belongs to insurance folk, 'cause dey are always considered pain in de butts till sometang goes wrong, den dey become de most important person in de family, I garontee.

De one "pain" 'round de bayou averybody try to dodge wan dey saw him comin' was ole Ducky Dubison, who sole insurance for Cajun National. He gots de name Ducky 'cause averybody wat seen him comin' would duck outta sight 'cause he was one of dem real pushy type salesman. Well, one day ole Emile Robichaw was up on top his house fixin' de roof, an' here come ole Ducky.

Ducky walk up an' say, "Come on down here, Emile, an' sign dat paper befo you do anytang else."

Emile say, "Wat paper, Ducky?"

Ducky say, "De paper dat's gonna gave you some insurance in case you got hurt up on top you house dere fixin' dat roof."

Emile say, "Ducky, I done span avery dime I got on material for dat roof, an' I can't ford to buy no insurance."

Ducky say, "Dat's wat I'm talk 'bout, Emile, an' why you gots to come sign dat paper."

Emile say, "Ducky, I don't got no time to waste, but I'm gonna took a minute to hear you 'splain why you would tole a man who jus' tole you he didn't have a dime to come sign a paper an' buy insurance from you wit' money he ain't got. Now 'splain dat."

Ducky say, "Well, Emile, I know dat almost averybody gots some can bury in de backyard or a cookie jar wit' a few extra dollar in it, ain't dat rite?"

Emile say, "I guess so."

Ducky say, "Well, jus' two months ago I talk ole Fontenot [pronounced Font In No] down de bayou into buy one of dem accident policy like I'm talk wit' you 'bout, an' won't you know, jus' lass week Fontenot was trim some tree an' fall out an' broke both his arm, both his leg, an' put a big crack in his back, an' I jus' brung him a check for $10,000, so who knows, next week or next month you might be de lucky one dat happens to, Emile."

De Gravediggers

Phillip Blanchard an' Clarence Theriot were always de lass two folks to say goodbye to anyone dat passed away in Breaux Bridge 'cause dey were de gravediggers in de Breaux Bridge cemetary. One day dey have de job of closin' de grave of a Broussard family member dat had pass away. As dey was shovelin', Clarence say, "Phillip, I heard a funny tang 'bout dis fella's family."

Phillip say, "Wat's dat?"

Clarence say, "Well, it seems dat de Broussard family always pass a $20 bill in de pocket of deir dearly departed so dey will have money to pay a toll charge if dey have one up at de River Jordan in Heaven."

Phillip say, "Yeah, I heard dat same tang Clarence, an' I only hope dis Broussard fella here could swim."

Clarence say, "Why's dat?"

Phillip say, "'Cause I got his $20 in my pocket, I garontee."

Jackson Square Cajun

If any of y'all aver been to New Orleans, hopefully you didn't miss out on a trip true Jackson Square to check out de work of some of de finest artist in de worl'. Dey also got fortune tellers, dancers, a statue of ole Andy Jackson on horseback, an' his worse enemies—de pigeons. In all dem tangs an' people de one fella I wanna focus on is ole Canvas Comeaux (pronounced Ko Moe), whose pictures look jus' like a snapshot he paints dem so good.

One day dis lady was walk all 'round de square an' pick ole Canvas to did de picture she want to gave her husband for his birthday. De lady go up an' start ax ole Canvas how much he would charge to paint a picture of her, for her husband. Canvas gave her de price an' dey both agree on dat, but jus' befo she walk off she say, "Oh, by de way, I did want dat picture paint nude. Does dat change de price?"

Canvas say, "No, mam, not one dime, but I gotta tole you one tang—I'm gonna have to kept my socks on or I won't have no ware to put my brushes."

TALL GAL

Ole Shorty Sonnier (pronounced Sewn Yea) have a date wit' dis gal who's nickname was Hoops 'cause she could play in de NBA she was so tall, but dat tall gal was sweet an' pretty, an' li'l 5'2" tall Shorty fine hisseff wantin' to kiss her real bad, so he axed her to took a walk wit' him down de bayou. While dey walk, Shorty mention to dat gal how bad he want to gave her a big kiss, an' she say she felt de same way, so Shorty spot dis cypress stump, an' he go grab it, an' lay it at dat tall gal's feet, step up on it, an' gave her dat kiss dey both wanted.

Later on dat evenin', afta dey had walked an' talked all day, Shorty walk dat girl home an' he axed her if she would mind gave him anodder one of dem big kiss. Dat tall gal say, "Shorty, dis is only our first date an' I don't know if I should let you kiss me again. I jus' don't know."

Shorty say, "Well, please made up you mind fass, cher, 'cause dis stump sure is gettin' heavy."

LIGHTEN' BUGS

It seems like de big city folk always love to made fun of us Cajuns. Likewise, us bayou folk always love to made fun of de city folk. De biggest thrill for either side is to get de odder on deir own turf an' out of deir natural habitat, an' dat's jus' wat happen de day dis fella from a big Chicago newspaper come down to Cajun Country to did a big report on life on de bayou. De guides de paper hired jus' happen to be Cush Cush Quibodeaux (pronounced Kwib Oh Do) an' his son, Gilbear, nicknamed "Grits," who's daughter an' sister had run off an' marry dis yankee fella who took her away from de bayou an' moved her way up north. Needless to say, love was not de word to describe deir feelin' for big-city folks.

Cush Cush an' Grits brung dat reporter fella back in de bayou to ware de mosquitos debate whether or not to eat you in de tent or took you outside ware de big mosquitos might took you. Well, dat night, jus' as dey blow out de lanterns an' settle down to sleep, one of dem lighten' bug dat had snuck by de tent screen door start flickerin' an', whoo yi yi, dat yankee reporter fella sit straight up an' yell, "Wat de worl' was dat?!"

They tole him, "Don't worry youseff 'bout dat, it was jus' a li'l mosquito bug flyin' round in de tent." Dat reporter come out de tent an' start pack his bag, beggin' Cush Cush an' Grits to please took him home. Dem two was grinnin' from ear to ear an' say, "Why? You afraid of a ole mosquito bug?"

De reporter, tryin' to save face say, "Not one li'l bit, but wan dey big 'nuff to come hunt you up wit' a flashlight, it's time to go home, I garontee!"

SAVIN' FACE

It was a sad day in Breaux Bridge wan ole T'Pratt passed away, 'cause he was well known an' loved by averybody. De funeral home was pack wit' people payin' deir lass respeck to T'Pratt an' his widow, Angelique.

De one tang nobody knew 'sept de funeral director, Guy B. Robear, an' Angelique is dat T'Pratt was bald as a eagle an' had always wore a wig his whole life. Angelique went to Guy B. befo de service cryin' an' worry dat on his lass day to be seen by anybody dat wig might fall off if somebody were to touch him while he was laid out. Guy B. assured Angelique dat would not happen in his funeral home an' for her not to worry one li'l bit.

Afta all de lass respecks was paid an' de funeral was over, T'Pratt's wig had stayed on his head an' not moved one li'l bit, jus' like Guy B. had promised. Angelique went down to de funeral home to pay for all de services an' handed Guy B. an' extra $50 for de big favor he had done for her T'Pratt.

Guy B. gave her back dat $50 an' say, "Oh no, mam, I couldn't took money from a poor widow woman like you. An' besides, dem few staples didn't cost me nothin'."

HOT

BACKSCRATCHER

My granpa tole me 'bout dis woman named Rona Barrio (pronounced Ba Re O), who always try to made people believe she was de queen of fashion, style, grace, an' etiquette, but de trueff of de matter is Rona nava went farther dan her mail box, much less travel de worl' like she want you to believe. De trueff came out 'bout Rona one day wan her husband, Ramsey, was workin' wit' ole Septieum Wiltz an' Septieum axed Ramsey, "How did Rona like dem li'l backscratcher tangs my wife sent her a few days ago?"

Ramsey say, "Sep, you don't know how glad I am dat you ax me dat question. Tank you so much for ax dat."

Sep say, "Ramsey, why you so happy 'bout me ax you dat question?"

Ramsey say, "Well, to tole you de trueff, I didn't have no idea in de worl' wat dem tangs were but Rona say she knew 'zackly wat dat was, an' she's been makin' me eat my salad wit' de new salad forks avery night dis week."

BAD DREAMS

I done mention averybody favorite doctor was ole Doc Duplichan, but wan you have mine trouble de only psychiatrist was Dr. Troyhorn. Granpa would always talk 'bout de time Shawee Borelle seen Dr. Troyhorn in town an' tole him 'bout dese bad dream he was havin'. Shawee say, "Doc, it's like dis. I go to sleep an' I get dis dream dat sometang terrible is unda my bed, an' I jump up, look unda dat bed, den all over de house, an' all night it's jus' like dat, avery two hour." Dr. Troyhorn say, "Shawee, I have more case jus' like wat you got, an' I taught I could done you some good wit' dem dream."

Shawee say, "How many visit you taught dat's gonna took, Doc?"

Dr. Troyhorn say, "Ain't no tellin', but usually 'bout three or four visit clear dat up."

Shawee say, "Well, Doc, how much dem visit cost?" Doc say, "'Bout $75 a piece."

Shawee's eyes open wide an' he could only say, "Tanks, I'll let you know," an' he left.

A few week pass an' Doc see Shawee in town an' axed, "When you gonna come see me?"

Shawee say, "Nava, Doc, 'cause I took care of dat problem, an' it didn't cost me but $10."

Doc say, "$10! Ain't no way you could get rid of dat problem witout talk wit' me."

Shawee say, "You wrong. I took care of dat trouble wit' a $10 ax." Doc say, "A ax?"

Shawee say, "Afta I axed de legs off de bed I ain't worry 'bout nothin' being unda dere no more!!!"

Fideaux's Diploma

One day ole Gilbear (Gilbert) LeBlanc was talkin' wit' Amos Guidry 'bout fishin', huntin', family, cookin', an' deir favorite subject of comparin' huntin' dogs. It seems dat for years de Bess Duck Huntin' Dog title was won by either Gilbear or Amos till Gilbear got Fideaux (Fido).

Gilbear say, "You know, Amos, I'll nava forgot de day li'l Emile start school an' Fideaux was jus' a puppy dat follow him, an' averyday an' avery year afta dat it become like one of dem how de call, tradition, dat Fideaux walk to school wit' Emile, but like all good tangs, dat come to an' end year befo lass."

Amos say, "Wat happen', Gilbear?"

Gilbear say, "Well, it seem like my boy Emile didn't did too good in school an' fail de 12th grade. But I'm gonna tole you, dat night at granulation, me an' Mama was so proud to be sit in de front row watchin' Fideaux walk cross dat stage an' got his diploma, I garontee."

Teachin' Fideaux

Fideaux was absolutely de finest duck-huntin' dog dat de bayou country had aver produced an' would aver see for de nex 100 year. De only tang dat Gilbear love more dan Fideaux was his family, an' he always took pride in sand his children to de bess schools wat money could buy, 'cause him an' his wife neither one have too much education.

When his oldest child, Emile, *finally* granulate from de high school, Gilbear start ax 'round wat was de bess "Big City College" dey could sand his boy Emile to, an' natural dat answer was LSU, in de capital city of Baton Rouge. Emile got to LSU an' fine out fass dat he love dat big city nightlife, but it coss a lot of money to did dat so he come up wit' a plan an' call his daddy. Emile say, "Daddy, here at LSU dey got one of dem animal professor dat tole me he could taught you Fideaux how to talk Franch, but dat's gonna coss you for $10,000."

Well, my frans, let me tole you, de taught of Fideaux did dat excite Gilbear an' he real quick tole Emile to be lookin' for Fideaux on de USP truck de nex day, 'cause he was gonna sand him special delivery 'long wit' de money. Sure 'nuff, here come de USP truck wit' ole Fideaux an' a suitcase wit' $10,000.

Well, I'm gonna tole you, Emile almost party hisseff to death wit' dat $10,000, but it all caught up to him wan it come time to go home for Christmas vacation an' he realize dat ole Fideaux hadn't learn Franch, so he put ole Fideaux on de nex slow boat to China, I garontee!

De whole family was waitin' for Emile to got home an' wan dey seen de car comin' averybody pile outside wit' ole man Gilbear pushin' averybody out de way yellin', "Y'all move an' let me talk Franch wit' my Fideaux." Wan he don't see him he say, "Emile, ware my dog? My Franch-talkin' Fideaux?"

Emile pull him off to de side an' say, "Daddy, I need to talk on you 'bout dat. I had to shoot ole Fideaux."

Whoo yi yi, wan he say dat de ole man's face turn red, you could fry an' egg on Gilbear's head it was so red hot, an' startin' to pop out wit' sweat. Wan he collect his mine he say, "You kill my $10,000 dog?! My Franch talkin' Fideaux?! Boy, you betta have a real good reason for kill my Fideaux or you gonna be in de behine of him, an' I mean rite now, too!"

Emile say, "Well, Daddy, it's like dis. Averytang was goin' fine, we was drivin' home, wan out de blue, Fideaux look up from de book he was readin' an' say, 'Hey, you 'magine de ole man is still goin' over to de widow Dupris [pronounced Dew Pre] avery Friday night wan he suppose to be at de Duck Huntin' Club Meetin'?"

Ole man Gilbear jump back an' say, "Boy, you did check twice to made for sure he was dead, huh?"

Milk Bass

Averybody dreams 'bout de day wan deir ship comes in, but few live to see de landin' like ole Sabre Labata an' his wife, O'Ta. Deir ship landed on November 15, 1968, wan oil was found on Sabre an' O'Ta's property.

Sabre tole O'Ta, "Cher, you been fine wife for 50 year, an' we been po folk for 50 year, too. Is dere anytang in dis worl' you aver did want dat I couldn't 'ford to gave you befo?"

O'Ta say, "Well, Sabre, dere is jus' one tang I always did want, an' dat is to took one of dem milk bass [baths] like I always heard 'bout dem rich lady took."

Sabre say, "Well, cher, if dat's wat you want we gonna took care of dat for you, I garontee."

So Sabre went down to see his fran Banny Fournier (pronounced Foun-Yea) at his grocery store an' tole him, "Banny, sole me 'nuff of dat milk for my wife O'Ta to took herseff one of dem milk bass like dem rich lady took."

Banny say, "O.K., Sabre, do you want dat milk pasteurized?"

Sabre say, "No, jus' sole me 'nuff to brung it up to her navel. She could splash it de ress of de way!"

De Three Leg Pig

Most Cajun folks quite simply refer to de folks livin' north of de Mason Dixon line as "dat yankee fella." One day a yankee fella was passin' true an' he stop off at de Dotrieve Autin (pronounced Oh Tan) Restaurant an' Scrap Metal Yard for a bite to eat. He kep heard averybody talkin' 'bout de three leg pig dis an' de three leg pig dat an' dat got his curiosity raised up so dat he finally axed Dotrieve ware dat three leg pig live. Dotrieve tole dat fella de pig belong to Stanley Barras, an' he tole him how to got to Stanley's farm.

Afta drivin' all 'round for two hour, dat yankee fella finally wine up at de Barras farm an' ole Stanley was up on de fron' porch rockin'. Dat yankee fella walk up to de porch an' axed, "Is dis de place ware dat three leg pig I been heard averybody talk 'bout live?"

Stanley say, "Oh yeah, my fran, you got de rite place. Wat could I help you wit'?"

Dat yankee fella say, "My fran, I wanna know—wat made dat pig so special?"

Stanley say, "Well, it's like dis. Year befo lass my youngest boy was playin' in de bayou wan he caught a cramp an' start to drown. Dat pig see dat an' go jump in an' grab my boy's arm an' swim him over to shore. If it wasn't for dat pig we would have loss dat boy."

Stanley went on to said dat lass year, wan averybody was sleepin', de house caught fire an' de pig notice dat fire an' he come buss down de door an' woke averybody up. Stanley say, "If it wasn't for dat pig, de whole family would have burned to death dat night."

Dat yankee fella say, "Whoo yi yi, dat is a special pig! Did he lose his leg in de fire?"

Stanley say, "No my fran, it wasn't de fire, it's jus' me. I can't stood de fack dat we would eat a pig like dat all at one time, I garontee."

At de Guardgate

Some folks can handle titles an' authority, but T. Bruce Broussard is definitely not one of dose people, I garontee. Averyone found dat out wan T. Bruce joined de Army an' dey decide to made him one of dem Military Police durin' his boot camp trainin', or as my grandpa Gilbert would say, "shoe camp" trainin'. His first post was to stan' guard at de base gate an' not to let nobody in unless dey have dis special sticker.

T. Bruce assured dem dat nobody was gonna get by him witout dat special sticker. Tangs at de gate were real slow an' dull an' ole T. Bruce was stood dere wavin' all de cars true till he spot dis car comin' dat don't got dat special sticker. Whoo, T. Bruce sprung into action an' jump out in de middle of de road wit' boat his hands out, an' yell at de top his voice, "*Hole on dere*, my fran, you can't come on dis base!"

The driver slam on de brakes an' T. Bruce say, "My fran, I'm Privates T. Bruce Broussard, an' you can't come on dis base 'cause you don't got dat special sticker on you car."

The driver say, "Look in de back seat." T. Bruce look an' dere sat a general wit' three stars on his shoulder. T. Bruce say, "I see, but dem star don't put dat sticker on you car."

Dat general say, "Boy, you see dem star? Dem star mean I could come on dis base or any odder base I care to go on, now you undastood dat!"

T. Bruce say, "General, hole averytang. Dis is my first day on de job an' I don't want to make any mistake. Tole me who I'm suppose to shoot—you or de driver?"

P.S. My granpa got a letter from T. Bruce rite afta dat say, "I nava taught no place could be colder dan huntin' in de bayou in winter, but de weather here in Iceland sure beats it, I garontee!"

OFF-BRAND RELIGION

Lorena an' René Hebert (pronounced A Bear) sent deir only child, li'l René, off to college, an' while he was dere he met de girl of his dreams, an' wrote de folks all 'bout dat girl. Well, it come round Christmas holiday time an' li'l René propose to dat girl an' she accept, so he got on de phone an' tole his mama he was gonna brung her soon-to-be daughter-in-law home for Christmas. Lorena got excite an' start name off all de special dishes she was gonna cook up for him an' dat daughter-in-law for Christmas dinner.

Li'l René say, "Mama, I got to tole you befo you do all dat, my fiancé is a vegetarian."

Well, folk, I gotta tole y'all po ole Lorena's heart almost stop, an' she cut dat phone talk off real short an' say, "O.K., we gonna be look for y'all in a few day, cher."

When Lorena hung up dat phone she brokes down in de biggest cryin' spell she aver have in her life. René come a runnin' to see wat de worl' done happen to made his Lorena brokes down like dat.

An' den afta he calm her down he say, "Cher, wat's wrong?"

Lorena say, "Oh, René, it's terrible, jus' terrible!" René say, "Wat's terrible, cher?"

Lorena say, "You know dat girl wat li'l René been wrote an' talk wit' us 'bout?"

René say, "Yea, wat 'bout dat girl?"

Lorena say, "He jus' brokes de news to me she ain't Catholic, Baptist, Methodist, or anytang I aver heard of. Dat girl is some kind of off-brand religion called 'Vegetarian'."

René say, "Hole averytang rite dere, cher, I believe it's worse dan you tink. I believe he was tellin' us dat girl can't have children an' we nava gonna be granparents, I garontee."

CHAPTER 12
Kids

QUESTIONS QUESTIONS

One day li'l Cush Cush Quibodeaux (pronounced Kwib Oh Do) axed his granma, "How ole you are?"

His granma say, "Whoo yi yi, boy, don't you nava ax a lady nothin' like dat!"

Den li'l Cush Cush say, "Well, Granma, how much do you weigh?"

De granma went to pieces an' say, "Whoo yi yi, cher, dat's worse dan ax a lady how ole she is. Don't nava ax nothin' like dat!"

De granma den tole li'l Cush Cush to stop ax her all dem questions an' go got hisseff some of dat candy she have in her purse.

Afta a while li'l Cush Cush come talk wit' his granma an' tole her, "Granma, I don't got to ax you no more question 'cause, wan I got dat candy, I fine out averytang 'bout you I wanna know."

De granma say, "Wat de worl' you talkin' 'bout, boy?"

Li'l Cush Cush say, "Well, Granma, wan I was in you purse I seen you driver's license an' I know how ole you are, I know how much you weigh, an', Granma, I know you got a 'F' in sex, too!"

FROG SOUNDS

One day old Gilbear (Gilbert) Wiltz's granson come prop hisseff up on his PawPaw's knee an' axed him to made a sound like a frog.

Gilbear was surprise at dat request an' axed him, "Cher, why in de worl' would you ax me to did somethin' like dat?"

De li'l granson say, "Well, PawPaw, I heard my daddy tole my mama dat wan you croak, we gonna be rich!"

THE END